The Day That

By
Kenneth Edward Barnes

Contents

Prologue

When the day began, it was just like any other. Or so it seemed. The sun had come up with its warm rays shining through the trees and into the bedroom window of the little cabin in the woods. Outside the window, birds are singing because spring has just begun. The daffodils have already burst through the ground and are in full bloom, their bright yellow blossoms are a welcoming sight after a long cold winter.

In the kitchen of the cabin, the sun is peeking through a window over the sink as a woman is putting on a pot of coffee. Above the sink, the clock says 8:35 A.M. as the woman goes to a cabinet, takes out two white cups and sets them on the table.

In the bedroom, her husband is just sliding out of bed and reaching for his pants, which are lying across a chair a few feet away. In a few minutes, they both will be sitting at the kitchen table having breakfast.

It is a Wednesday morning and the couple has been looking forward to the coming weekend. Both are tired from the many hours they've spent working around the cabin, but have finally gotten everything they wanted to do done. To reward themselves they decide to take a very long and deserved five-day weekend. They just want to stay at home and enjoy the next few days of early spring.

This day, however, will not be like any the couple has ever known. For that matter, it will be unlike anything that has ever happened throughout the entire world. It will be a day that time stood still!

What makes this day different?

Why is it important?

Half way around the world an event will happen that will cause worldwide panic. Everyone on earth will be thrust into chaos such as it has never known. What is this event? What is the chaos? This story will tell you. The most surprising thing is—much of this book is not fiction, but fact!

Chapter 1

The Day the Clock Stopped

The date is the morning of April 6, 2033, at 8:35 Central Standard Time somewhere in Southern Indiana just a few miles north of the Ohio River.

On a hillside within a mile of the Hoosier National Forest, is a small cabin. Inside is fifty-six-year-old Janet Blackburn. Living with her is her husband, sixty-three-year-old Robert.

Janet is an attractive brunette, rather tall and slender but with enough curves to please her husband. She wears glasses, and has a warm smile and green eyes that show the kindness and compassion she has in her heart. She and Rob have only been married for two years but she feels lucky to have found such a man after she became a widow four years earlier. Now she has a new love of her life.

Rob is a strong man in body and in spirit. He is rather slender, but muscular. Atop his partially balding head, he usually wears a faded cap. What hair he has is nearly white and he wears a well-trimmed matching beard. Rob, too, was a widower after he lost his precious wife, Karen. She died suddenly from a heart attack and left him alone five years earlier.

Rob retired from his teaching career only ten months before and has been working on their vacation cabin since that time. Up until then, Rob was a biology teacher at a local high school. He loved his job because he loved teaching children about nature. He worked as a schoolteacher until he turned sixty-two. For the past several months, he has been semi-retired. After he left teaching, he began writing some outdoor columns in local newspapers and even had a few nationally published stories in some outdoor magazines.

It was Rob's dream to live in a cabin in the woods when he retired. He bought the property seven years earlier and built the small cabin himself. It was off the grid so he installed solar panels along with several large batteries so he and Karen could have electricity. He also had dug a well, which supplied fresh drinking water from a deep spring. Inside the house, they had running water, all propane appliances: cooking stove, space heater, hot water tank and refrigerator. They would have no monthly bills except for food and twice a year the 500-gallon propane gas tank would need to be filled. They were pretty much self-sufficient.

Also, on the property, Rob had planted several kinds of fruit trees along with a few nut trees. In the backyard, they had a small garden and even a chicken house. Rob wanted to have fresh eggs when they retired and planned the space for half a dozen hens. Their place was like a mini farm and both of them loved it.

Then, when he thought things could not get much better, Karen suddenly left him. Rob was crushed. He had his dream, yet it meant nothing without someone there to share it. Karen was only fifty-five years old when she died and Rob thought it wasn't fair. It had long been his dream to retire with Karen at his side. Now he had to go on without her and at times, the loneliness was almost unbearable. After the loss of his beloved wife, Rob was more determined than ever to finish the house he had started for Karen. He did it more for her than himself, but he needed something to occupy his time until the grief subsided. Karen had loved the cabin and looked forward to the day they both could live in it permanently. Up until the day she died, they only were able to stay in it on weekends and during vacations.

Although she was never to realize her dream, she did die at the place she loved. Rob had held her as she drew her last breath inside the cabin.

It happened one day in early May. As Rob was putting some shelves in the closet, Karen was outside working, planting the flowers she loved. She had planted several tubs of Impatiens and Petunias after which she hung her hummingbird feeders on the front porch. She also loved hummingbirds and could hardly wait until they arrived in late April or early May. Suddenly Rob heard her call out for him. Rushing to the front door, he saw Karen clutching her left shoulder and trying to come in the front door. Taking her in his arms, he only had a few moments with her before she was gone. Her heart had stopped without warning. That morning they had awakened together full of life and joy. Before the morning was over, Rob had lost his entire world.

A year after Karen passed away, Rob met Janet. It seemed to be destiny. She was also a widow and had recently moved to a nearby town. She just happened to attend the same church one day and when they met, it was as if they had known one another for years. They had so much in common.

Janet loved nature and once she discovered Rob would soon be retiring and living in a cabin in the woods, she was intrigued. She had grown up on a farm, but her husband always wanted to live in town. She had missed the smell of hay fields and the crowing of a rooster each morning. She often had a few tomato plants even in the city, but it was not the same as having a real garden.

She, like Rob, had suddenly lost her husband. For her, life changed suddenly one afternoon when he was driving home from work. After stopping by the grocery store for a carton of eggs and a gallon of milk, he was coming through town near a construction site. Janet had called and asked him if he would mind stopping at the store, so she would not have to make a special trip. He never made it home. A heavy, laden dump truck had run a traffic light and hit his car—killing him instantly. She had blamed herself for asking him to stop at the store. If he had not gone there, he would not have been at the intersection when the truck ran the red light. She knew in her heart that her husband did not blame her. He would have told her it was just one of those things if he could. That, however, did not take away the loneliness she felt with him gone.

Both Rob and Janet loved to talk and share their feelings about life, love and their aspirations for the future. Neither one had children, and they loved kids, but that part of their life was over. They did not like being alone and when they were together they felt complete. Naturally, it didn't take long before Rob and Janet were deeply in love. No longer did either one of them take life for granted. They did not want to take any chances at losing in a split second what they'd found with one another. They decided not to waste time on a long engagement, and they were soon married. Rob was happier than he'd been for a long time and so was Janet.

Janet looks younger than her age. She could pass for an attractive forty-year-old. Rob has also taken care of himself. With all the work, he has done on clearing the land for his cabin, and with the time and energy he spent on building his dream home, his body is in very good shape, and it shows. He does have a hearing loss, which he's had since he was a child. Janet also had injured her back several years earlier when she had fallen from a ladder in her own kitchen. She also has a minor problem with her blood pressure. Other than this, they are in good health. They are both very lucky and they know it.

The morning they had just gotten out of bed, Rob had been putting the finishing touches on the cabin and the yard. Both had been living in the cabin shortly after Rob retired. In the past week, he has put up their mailbox, bought some young chickens and planted a couple of pink dogwood trees to make the yard look even better. Rob has also put up a large bird feeder. Janet loves to watch the birds outside the kitchen window. Everything is finally done and the place looks picturesque.

Rob has already sold the house that he and Karen had lived in most of their married life. Janet was living in an apartment before marrying Rob. Now the cabin will be their home for the rest of their lives.

Their small cabin is well off the grid as there are no powerlines or phone lines nearby. They must use cell phones to communicate with the outside world, but they can get several television stations, which they often watch in the evenings.

The cabin sits on the side of a hill on twelve acres of mostly wooded land. The property runs between a gravel road to the north and a small stream to the south. The stream then runs into a larger creek about a half mile from their house. There is a small garden at the edge of the yard and Rob has a large shed where he keeps his tools and lawn mowers. He also has a small chicken house for the young hens and rooster he has recently bought. It is a beautiful place.

As soon as Rob is dressed that morning, he comes into the kitchen where Janet is preparing breakfast. Seeing her getting some large brown eggs from the refrigerator, he said, "I'll be glad when our chickens are laying. They will lay large brown eggs just like those."

Janet turns to him, "You do want two this morning, don't you?"

"Yeah, two is fine, sweetheart. I would like a couple of beef sausage links and a couple slices of toast, too, if you don't mind."

"You're certainly hungry this morning, aren't you?" she said, with a coy grin.

He knows why she was smiling. "Sure, I'm hungry. I spent a lot of energy last night. Don't you remember?"

"How could I forget? You were terrific," she replied, as she breaks the eggs into a frying pan.

"You sounded as if you enjoyed it," he said, looking into her green eyes.

"Oh, I did," she said, as she comes over to give him a kiss.

As she bends over to kiss him, he notices she still has her nightgown on under the blue cotton robe. He had gotten her the nightgown on her last birthday and she always looks very sexy in it. It is low cut in the front and as she bends over to kiss him, she gives him a good close-up view of her cleavage. The kiss lasts longer than he expected too, and he has to interrupt her.

"I love your kisses, sweetheart. But if you don't stop, we'll have to go back into the bedroom and I don't know if I have the energy."

"Okay." Janet smiles and turns to go back to preparing breakfast. "I'll fix you breakfast so you can build up your strength. I can't have my man too weak to take care of his husbandly duties," she says giggling.

"I enjoy performing my husbandly duties," he said, as he watches her put two pieces of bread in the toaster.

"You always seem to enjoy doing them," she said, glancing over her shoulder at him.

As Rob is sitting there, he happens to look up at the clock above the sink. "I thought it was later than that."

Janet looks up at the clock and said, "It looks as if it has stopped. I think it said the same time when I first came in the kitchen."

"Must be the battery. I thought I put a new one in just about a month ago. Maybe it's not getting a good connection. I'll check it after breakfast."

After enjoying their eggs, sausage and toast, they sit at the table and talk about how beautiful the morning is as they sipped on their second cup of coffee. When Rob finishes his coffee, Janet begins putting the dishes in the sink to wash them. "Don't wash them yet, honey, until I check that clock," Rob said. "I'll have to put a chair in front of the sink to reach it."

"I'll go get a new battery in case it needs one," Jan said.

"Okay," he said, pulling a chair up to the sink. Stepping on the chair, he reaches up and takes down the clock. After stepping back down, he turns around, sits down, and begins checking to see if the battery is getting a good connection.

"Huh," he said. "It seems to be good and tight. It must be the battery."

By this time, Janet has come back into the kitchen with a fresh battery. "Here, honey," she said, handing it to him.

"Thank you, sweetheart."

Taking the old one out, he hands it to Janet and slides the new battery into place. Rob then turns it over to see if it is running.

"What's wrong with it?" Janet asked.

"I don't know. The clock is not very old. I bought it only about a year ago. The battery I took out looked okay, there wasn't any corrosion around the contacts."

"Do you want to try another battery?" asked Jan.

"I don't think it would do any good. I know it's possible that a new battery could be bad, but it hardly seems likely," he said, looking up at her. "Have we got any more?"

"I think that was the last new one. I can get one out of the other clock in the bedroom just to check to see if it's the clock or the battery."

"Go ahead," Rob said, as he keeps fooling with the battery trying to get it to work.

About a minute later, his wife comes back into the kitchen.

Looking up from the clock, Rob sees Janet standing there with a battery in her hand but with an odd expression on her face.

"You have another battery?" he questions, seeing it in her hand.

"Yes, but I don't think it will do any good."

"Why is that?"

"The clocks in the bedroom have stopped, too."

"They have stopped?" Rob said, with surprise. "What do you mean?"

"Yeah, and they've stopped at 8:35. When I started to get the clock off the wall, I saw that it had stopped. So, I went over to the nightstand by your side of the bed to the little travel clock and it has stopped, too.

"That's crazy. How can three clocks have stopped at the exact same time? The batteries could not run down all at the very same moment!"

"It's more than crazy. Look at this," Janet said, as she holds up her wrist watch."

Taking it from her, he looks down at the hands and they are sitting at 8:35! "What in the world is going on?" Rob exclaimed. "This can't be real!"

"I don't know."

Putting the kitchen clock on the sink beside him, Rob goes to the bedroom and picks up his wristwatch. He is almost afraid to look at it, but he does. Disbelief comes over him as it, too, says 8:35!

"What's going on Rob?" Janet said, as she steps into the bedroom.

"I don't know," he answered, looking up at her with deep concern on his face. "Why don't you call your sister and see if something strange is going on at their house."

Walking into the living room, Janet picks up her phone, Rob is right behind her.

"It's on," she said, "but there's no signal."

"Maybe the cell tower's down."

"Honey," Janet said, looking up from her phone. "The phone's on, but there's no time displayed!"

"My Lord!" Rob exclaimed. "I'll turn the TV on and see if there's any news. It sounds like maybe there's been a solar flare or something that has knocked out the electronics."

"Or a nuclear attack," Janet said, her voice breaking.

Picking up the remote, Rob turns towards the TV. As he does, he sees that the DVR is flashing 12:00 o'clock A.M. "The DVR is on, but it has lost the time. Something strange is sure going on," he said, as he pushes the on button for the television.

They both stand there, nearly holding their breath, afraid of what they might soon discover. The television comes on, and to their surprise, the morning news is on.

"Well, that's a relief," Rob said, with a smile. "At least we have a TV signal."

"Yeah," Janet said. "I was beginning to worry that there had been some kind of catastrophe."

Rob turns up the volume as he stares in disbelief. The news anchor seems upset and behind him, a video is being broadcast about something that has just happened. Rob notices that the clock on the wall behind the reporter said it is 9: 45. "The clocks are working there," he said.

As they stand there in the living room, they listen as a field reporter begins speaking. He is standing on the street in what looks like a Middle Eastern country.

"A little more than an hour ago we witnessed something remarkable," the reporter said, his face somber and appearing to be troubled.

"That's when our clocks stopped," Janet said.

"Wait, honey. Let's hear what's going on."

The reporter continues as video is being shown and soon they both know what has just taken place.

"Oh, my God!" exclaimed Rob. "This can't be happening!"

Chapter 2

In the "Nick" of Time

To understand what has just happened we must go back three and a half years before this day. Even when Rob and Janet learn the truth, they will not fully understand the implications of why their world and their time have stood still. As time goes on, however, it will slowly dawn on them that the most remarkable events are yet to come.

To understand why the clock has stopped and what they witnessed we must go back even further. Several years before this monumental event took place, terrorism had escalated to an all-time high. Europe was flooded with refugees, many of which had come just to infiltrate the peaceful society and launch terrorists' attacks from within. Not only were the attacks happening in Europe, but around the world. America, as well as Russia, China, Australia, India and a host of other countries were living in fear.

There had recently been a meeting of the European countries to try to find a way to stop the violence. Not only were the terrorists wreaking havoc in the lives of the citizens of the countries of Europe, but also there was the threat of Russia. The Soviet Union was rising again and were flexing their military muscles, threating to take back many of the eastern countries that had recently joined Europe. All this uncertainty was causing their shaky economies to further deteriorate and were on the edge of collapse.

The leaders of Europe knew they must join as never before to confront the threats from within and from without.

At a secret meeting, the leaders of ten European countries were present: Germany, Italy, France, Spain, Greece, Austria, Belgium, Finland, Denmark and the Netherlands.

The euro had recently lost much of its value. After England pulled out of the European Union in 2016, some other countries followed suit. Greece went bankrupt, as did several other countries. Germany had to bail them out and now all of them stood on the threshold of either collapsing or uniting as never before. The terrorists' attacks had people living in constant fear. Bombs and coordinated attacks had killed thousands just in the past two years. Europe had opened its doors to the refugees and many from the war-torn nations saw their chance of coming in and invading without having to fight a war to get there. The people of Europe had had enough. There were demonstrations and riots every day in the streets. Many of the people began to fight back. They did not want people in their country, which did not want to be Europeans but wanted to change the country to be like the ones the refugees had just come from.

The leaders knew they had to do something and do it soon before there was an all-out civil war.

At the meeting was also the newly elected Pope. The leaders believed that perhaps the faith of the people could be the glue that would hold the many nations together. The new pope was unlike any before him. He had the name of Peter the Roman and he was from Italy. For centuries, all the popes came from Italy, then for many years, none came from there. Now Pope Peter had just been elected from Italy once again. The pope had spoken out against what he saw as persecution of the faithful Christians by the Islamic terrorists. He said he was a man of peace, but the church had a right to defend the helpless. He called upon the countries to unite to fight the scourge of radical Islamic terrorism. He

16

said he did not want a war, but they had declared war on him and his followers.

The leaders of Europe thought this just might be what the countries needed. There was also a new leader in Italy. He was a young man whose closest friends knew as "Nick". His full name was Nickolas Romero Romulus. Chancellor Romulus seemed to have the answers to a host of problems the countries were facing. He was also very charismatic and seemed to have an inner power that caused people to want to follow him. Chancellor Romulus agreed that the Pope could play a needed role in forming a stronger bond. In the past, the church had been instrumental in guiding the countries in the right direction.

This new leader with a charming and magnetic personality advised that what the counties needed, besides the church to guide them, was one strong leader. If all the countries would get behind one leader, and act as one, then it would be an invincible union. They all agreed.

They also agreed that this new leader of Italy take control. He was young, very bright and had great charisma. Just the thing the countries needed.

At the meeting, they had a vote and it was unanimous that the new leader of Italy, Chancellor Nickolas Romulus, be the head of a New Unified Europe. After they had agreed, they asked him to speak to those assembled.

Walking to the podium in front of the room, he turns to address the other European leaders. With a warm smile, he begins, "Ladies and gentlemen, and Holy Father. We need not only to go in a new direction—we need something that will work."

All those around the table nod their heads.

"Many empires have come and gone, but one endured for centuries," he said, as he looks around the room. "It was never conquered and could not have been, but for one reason. It decayed from within because the people lost their will to stay united and because it grew too large to govern itself. Now if we revive this empire once again, but this time make sure we stay strong it will again be invincible. Today we have instant communications, which was something we did not have two thousand years ago. Now we can unify our people as never before. For we have a cause, we have the will—and soon we will have the power.

"We can have this power and prestige by having a military that will keep the peace. We can do this by using the church and the faith that held the empire together for hundreds of years. We will then not have to fear that any other country or even a host of countries can threaten our borders or terrorize our citizens ever again. We can! We must! And we will—bring the Roman Empire back from the pages of history to fulfill its destiny!"

The people erupt in applause and stand to their feet.

As soon as they take their seats, the Chancellor continues, "I feel it is also my destiny to lead it to glory once again. It will be even more glorious than before and someday it shall rule the world!"

"What will we call this new Roman Empire?" someone asked.

"It was once called Imperial Rome, and I believe that is a fitting name once again," he said, looking at the Pope. "Yes, Imperial Rome will rise from the ashes as did the legendary Phoenix of old!

Chapter 3

A Time for Peace!

After the leaders emerged from the meeting, they were all smiles. Chancellor Romulus immediately called all the military leaders of the ten European countries together and had a closed-door meeting.

The United States had already begun withdrawing troops from around the world. Their economy could not sustain a military presence in Europe, Japan, or South Korea. They had fought terrorism for many years, which had drained their resources and their will to keep fighting. They wanted and needed other countries to take over the battle against terrorism.

In only months, Germany began cranking out military weapons as never before. The other countries supplied money and manpower to help make them the strongest military power on earth. The new Imperial Rome soon began to have pride and prestige that they hadn't had since ancient times.

At the same time, the Islamic countries began to become frightened. The radical Islamic factions began to think they had bit off more than they could chew and decided to quit fighting amongst themselves and also unite. Iran was the largest country with the greatest number of military weapons. This would be their rallying point. They would follow suit and become a great military power that would rival Imperial Rome. Iran had already developed several small nuclear weapons and had threatened to use them if necessary. This however only made Rome more determined to build up their strength.

Within two years, the New Roman Empire had enough weapons produced that no country on earth would dare challenge them. That is except for one. The United Islamic States began making threats of cutting off the oil supply to the European countries. They had already blackmailed several other countries into paying exorbitant amounts for their oil.

This did not go over well with the new leader of Rome. Chancellor Romulus had to show the world that he was a leader to be reckoned with. In an unprecedented move, he launched a three-pronged attack on Egypt, Libya and Iran. Almost overnight those countries were crushed and were wanting peace. Hundreds of thousands of military personnel as well as civilians had been killed in the bombings. The leaders were also targeted and every leader of the United Islamic States was taken out. Fear quickly swept not only throughout the Islamic nations, but also around the world. The entire world knew the New Roman Empire was not to be taken lightly.

Soon after this blitzkrieg of the Middle East, Chancellor Romulus visited Israel. No one had been able to bring peace to that region since Israel became a nation in 1948. Seeing his chance after his recent conquest of the Islamic countries, he believed it was time to settle things.

Within a month, the United Islamic States had chosen new leaders that were willing to listen to reason and to bring peace to their devastated countries.

A meeting was then held in Jerusalem by Chancellor Romulus to broker a peace agreement between Israel and the United Islamic States. Israel's Prime Minister was David Shalom. As his name implied, he was a man that wanted peace. He had not been able to get the old leaders of the United Islamic States to come to the table to talk peace.

They had been set on Israel's destruction. Now things had changed, for Israel had someone fighting for them.

It was right before one of Israel's most Holy Days, Yom Kippur when Chancellor Romulus met with David Shalom and the new leaders of the United Islamic States. The meeting did not last but four hours and when the leaders emerged, they were all smiles.

A press conference was held immediately afterwards and the world watched with anticipation.

As Chancellor Romulus stepped up to the microphone behind the podium, he had the Israeli Prime Minster on his right and the leader of the United Islamic States, Sheik Mohamad Omar, on his left.

"I have good news," Chancellor Romulus said. "We have reached a peace agreement."

He was interrupted by an enthusiastic applause.

Motioning for the people to calm down so he could continue he smiled. "Prime Minister Shalom and Sheik Omar have agreed to a seven-year peace agreement. During this time, all sides will begin disarming."

Again, he was interrupted by applause.

It took a minute or so before the shouts and whistles died down so he could begin speaking again.

"Besides disarmament, Israel has agreed to withdraw from some of the occupied land in exchange for something they have not had in over 2,000 years." He pauses, looks over the crowd then smiles, "We have agreed that they should have a third temple in which to worship!"

A hush came over the news media. No one could believe this man had been able to do such a thing. Then a news reporter in the front spoke up, "Where will it be built, Chancellor Romulus?"

"Right here in Jerusalem—beside the Dome of the Rock. Islam has three sites they consider Holier that this site, therefore I thought it only fair that the people of Israel have a temple on their most Holy site."

Instantly everyone was trying to ask questions, but Chancellor Romulus just smiled and held up his hands to make them quite down once again. He knew what their questions were but he already had the answers before they asked.

"I have promised Prime Minister Shalom that every nation will contribute to the construction of the new temple. It will be the most beautiful building on earth. It will make Solomon's Temple or King Herold's Temple seem small and insignificant."

"How long will it take to build such a temple?" a woman reporter asked.

"I'm not sure, but we will not rush it. It will be a building that will stand for ten thousand years!"

Chapter 4

Just in Time!

Three and a half years later, the temple in Jerusalem was nearing completion and just in time. The holy Feast of Passover was nearing and everything for the third temple was ready to resume where things had left off nearly 2,000 years before. The last time a sacrifice was made was in 70 A.D., just before the Romans destroyed King Herald's temple.

The priests for the temple had already been selected; all of their garments were made years ago in anticipation of this day, as were most of the articles that went inside.

Then three weeks before Passover, Chancellor Romulus came to Jerusalem to meet with the Prime Minister. He said he had a "great announcement" to make.

No one knew what he had in mind. He said it was a secret but the world would be astounded.

At 10 A.M. local time, his private jet touched down in Tel Aviv. As he stepped off the plane, news reporters from around the world were waiting with cameras ready.

Coming down the stairs of the plane, he was all smiles and began waving to those that were gathered. Reaching the bottom of the stairs, he held up his hand to hush the dozens of questions that the news people were shouting at him. A hush soon came over the crowd as he spoke.

"I am glad to be here today. As I promised," he said, as he glanced over the people, "I have an announcement that will stun the world." As he spoke, there suddenly appeared in the door of the plane, the Pope. The crowd was more than surprised.

The Chancellor turned to look up at the Pope as the Pontiff began coming down the stairs. "No, that is not the announcement," he said. "I wanted the Pope here with me because what I will tell you will rekindle your faith—Jew and Christian alike. It will be something the world is not prepared for."

Everyone was stunned and began asking one another what he could have in mind.

When the Pope reached the bottom of the stairs, he whispered something to the Chancellor and they both smiled. Chancellor Romulus turned to the reporters and said, "We will have the announcement right after lunch in front of the New Temple. I'm told it will begin at 2 o'clock local time."

At that moment, the Chancellor's motorcade pulls up next to him and he and the Pope get inside the long black Limousine and are whisked away.

By fifteen minutes before 2 o'clock, everyone has gathered in front of the magnificent third temple.

Chairs have been placed in front of a podium and everyone from the press, as well as some international dignitaries are already seated.

Other chairs have been placed behind the podium for the Chancellor, the Pope and Prime Minister Shalom.

About five minutes before 2, the Prime Minister walks out of the temple with the Chancellor and the Pope. Chancellor Romulus and the Pope take a seat as the Prime Minister steps up to the podium.

Looking over the crowd, he smiles, glances back at the Pope and Chancellor, then back to the crowd once more. After a brief pause, he begins to address those that are there.

"Ladies and gentlemen, foreign dignitaries, and honored guests. I do not know what Chancellor Romulus has to announce, but I'm sure it will be important. If it were not for him, we would not be standing here today in front of the most magnificent building on earth. We, the people of Israel and the world, wish to thank him for his great wisdom in achieving what no other has been able to do. Chancellor Romulus is a man with vison and a man of peace. He has demonstrated his heartfelt desire to make the world a better place for all people. We are all very anxious to hear what he has to say. So, without any further ado, here is the man we have been waiting for, Chancellor Nickolas Romero Romulus!"

With that, the Prime Minister steps to the side as the Chancellor comes to the podium.

Not a word or whisper is spoken as everyone is waiting to hear him speak. Only the clicking of cameras is heard as he looks over the crowd and smiles. "Ladies and gentlemen, I have had you gather today to make an announcement that will shock the world. As the Prime Minister said, I am a man of peace. The Holy City of Jerusalem is also known as the city of peace. Many prophets and men with vision and courage have come to this place over the span of many centuries. Great men of the past have come and stood where I am standing today. Solomon with his great wisdom and glory built the first temple. Herald the Great was responsible for making the second temple, one of the greatest buildings of the world. Sadly, it was the Roman Empire that destroyed the second temple. Now the New Roman Empire has built a much greater one.

"You have seen the outside of this great temple and it is indeed splendid, but you have not seen the inside. I can tell you it is far more majestic and magnificent on the inside than what you can see here today. In a matter of days, everyone in the world will have the opportunity to see its glory when it is dedicated.

"As grand as it is, there is something missing. It was there in Solomon's great golden temple, but it was not there in the second temple in Herald's time. Handed down to me from those great men of the long ago, is a secret knowledge. A secret that has been hidden for twenty-five hundred years!"

The Chancellor turns and looks at the Pope as the Pope stands and walks to his side. "I would rather show you than tell you," Chancellor Romulus said, as he and the Pope look over the crowd. The Chancellor then looks behind him as four men come out of the temple doors rolling something that is covered in a tan canvas tarp.

With the Pope beside him, the Chancellor walks to the tarp and nods for the men that have brought it out to leave. Then with the Pope, takes hold of the tarp, lifts it, and takes it from what is beneath. Instantly there are gasps. A woman in the front faints. News reporters are so shocked that they cannot speak and the camera crews have difficulty focusing their cameras on what they see.

The Chancellor and the Pope turn to the crowd once more as Chancellor Romulus smiles and said, "Ladies and gentlemen, I present to you the *Ark of the Covenant!*"

Everyone is stunned. The Ark has been missing before the Babylonians took the Jews into captivity five hundred years before Christ. There have been rumors since that time that it was hidden in many places. Jeremiah the prophet was supposed to have hidden it under the orders of God himself, but no one knew where it was. Now this man has said he has known its whereabouts for many years and the knowledge has been handed down to him.

The Pope then steps to the podium. "I wanted to say a few words. Chancellor Romulus is no ordinary man as many of you have already guessed. He has known where the Ark has been hidden all his life, as have I. The secret has been passed down since the day it was hidden to certain special people. It could not be brought out into the light until the time was right. The time is now right. The third temple is complete and the Chancellor has brought world peace.

Therefore, it is time to place the Ark back where it should be and that is in the Holy of Holies inside the new temple."

Suddenly someone in the crowd yells out, "He is the long-awaited Messiah!"

"The Messiah?" a news reporter said.

"Yes," another said, "he has brought peace when no one else could. He has protected Israel and built us a temple. Only the Messiah could do that."

Everyone was talking as the camera crews were trying to get close up pictures of the Ark

The Chancellor, however, motioned for the four men that had brought it out to cover it once again and take it back inside the temple.

As soon as it is out of sight, Prime Minister Shalom steps up to the podium to once again address those that are gathered. Looking over to the Chancellor and the Pope, which have taken their seats, he said, "Chancellor Romulus, we would be honored if you would be the man to dedicate the new temple on our Passover."

The Chancellor nods, "I would be most honored and humbled to do so."

The news flashes around the world. It is almost unbelievable. Not only is a third temple just complete, but the Ark of the Covenant has been discovered after twenty-five hundred years! It is the news of the century; no, it is the news of the millennium!

Joy was in not only Jerusalem, but also all around the world. Peace had finally come. The world had never seen anything like it. Everyone was looking forward to the day that Chancellor Romulus would dedicate the new temple.

Chapter 5

It's Time

There is more joy in the world than anyone can ever remember. Strangers say hello to one another. Divorces stop. Crime is almost nonexistent. There are no wars anywhere in the world. Not even a conflict. Those that have left their native countries are coming back. They have been doing so ever since the Chancellor brought peace. Those that have fled their war-torn countries in the past feel that it is safe to return home. Broken families are reunited. It is a time like no one had even dreamed was possible. Prosperity, joy, and a feeling of security has swept around the world. Suicides have even come to a halt. Many in prison have been set free to commemorate the great day.

Passover is fast approaching and people are finding it difficult to wait.

Ten days before the dedication is to take place, the Ark of the Covent is moved into the place it has been missing since ancient days. It is placed behind a thick royal blue curtain in the Holy of Holies. The elected High Priest is Joseph Aaron. As soon as four other priests have it sitting it in its rightful place, Joseph comes in to uncover it. The canvas tarp that was draped over it at the announcement of its discovery still hides what lies beneath. Upon uncovering the Ark, Joseph, as well as the other priests, are amazed at what they see.

Besides the beauty of the ancient box and the two golden angels that are at each side holding their wings above the Ark, the men see something else.

28

One of the priests steps forward and looks at the Mercy Seat. What he sees here is what has caught their attention. The priest looks over at Joseph. "It seems the last time the Ark was in Solomon's Temple no one cleaned the blood from the Mercy Seat, "he said. "Should I get something and clean it off?"

Joseph is stunned because he knows if it was used in Solomon's Temple the blood would not be there. "No, wait," he said, stroking his beard as he stares at the thick brown stain. "Let me think about this for a moment,"

"Where was the Ark found?" asked another priest.

"I was told it was found hidden under Golgotha," said another.

"The Place of the Skull?" said the third priest. "That's where Christ was said to have died."

"Yeah, I know," Joseph, replied.

"It couldn't be," but Joseph cuts him off.

"It could be," Joseph said, looking up from the Ark. "It very well could be." He then said, "Go to my chambers, get the letter opener on my desk, and bring a sheet of paper. I'm going to get a sample and see what kind of blood it is."

A few minutes later, the priest is back and Joseph carefully scrapes a small sample from the Mercy Seat onto the sheet of paper and folds it so it will not spill. "I'm going to the hospital lab and have this blood checked. We will soon know if it is the blood of a bull, a lamb or a man."

Soon Joseph was on his way to the hospital. After meeting with the director of the hospital, they both go down stairs and Joseph gives the blood sample to the lab technician.

"Be extremely careful with that sample," Joseph said, as he hands it to the young man. "I want to know what kind of blood it is. It could be of extreme historical importance."

"Yes, sir," the young man said. "I'll be extra careful."

"I'll be at the temple," Joseph said to the director. "As soon as something is found, please call me."

"I'll call as soon as the lab work is finished. It should be complete before the day is over."

Later that afternoon, Joseph receives a call on his cell phone. "Joseph, this is Jacob. We have the lab tests completed."

"What did you find?" asks Joseph with great anticipation.

"I think you better come down here. You... you won't believe what we found."

"I'll be right there," Joseph said, running out the door.

Fifteen minutes later, Joseph is met at the lab by the lab technician and Jacob.

After greeting one another again, Jacob looks at Joseph, "Let's go into the lab, Joseph. I want to show you something."

All three men come inside and Jacob shuts the door behind them. "Come over here," Jacob said to Joseph, "I want you to see something."

Going over to a desk where a computer is sitting, the lab technician sits down and brings up a screen with a graph displayed.

"Look at this, Joseph," Jacob said, pointing to the screen. "The blood is human and is type A Positive."

"Human blood? That's hard to believe," Joseph said, with a puzzled expression.

"Yes, but that's not all. Once we determined that it was human blood, we had the DNA analyzed. A normal person has 46 pairs of chromosomes, 23 from the mother and 23 from the father. A normal man has 23 pairs of chromosomes with one Y chromosome. This blood has 47 pairs of chromosomes with two Y chromosomes!"

"What does that mean?" Joseph asked looking up at Jacob mystified.

"It means that this blood came from a man that had no earthly father."

"My God!" exclaims Joseph.

"My God is correct," Jacob says astoundingly.

"You mean this blood may have come from Christ?" said Joseph.

"That's the only conclusion I can come up with," an astonished Jacob says.

"I don't know what to say," Joseph appears flabbergasted.

"I would tell no one, because no one will believe you," Jacob said, with great caution in his voice.

Joseph is stunned. "Could it be true?" he thought. "Was our Messiah here? Had he died just as the Christian Bibles said he did?"

Joseph knew Christ's Hebrew name was Yeshua, which means *Salvation*. He also knew that the letters in the Hebrew alphabet also stand for words. The words in Yeshua's name says, *"See the nail in God Almighty's hand!"* His mind was reeling from what the implications of what he has discovered might mean.

After leaving the hospital, Joseph thought he should do as Jacob said and tell no one. If it truly was Christ's blood, then it is in God's hands. As he thought on it, things began to become clear to him. Christ had died on the cross directly above where the Ark was hidden. The Gospels said there was a great earthquake as he died and it tore the temple veil in two. It must have also opened the cracks in the rocks beneath the cross. When his side was pierced, the blood and water gushed out and some of it ran down into the rocks and dripped onto the Mercy Seat several feet below. When he said this, a picture suddenly came flashing his mind. There was a wine and water pouring ceremony, which he did every year at Sukkot. Two men would stand before the congregation. One would pour wine from a bottle as the other poured water. The wine and water would mix as it poured onto the ground. It was a picture of Christ's blood pouring out on to the ground when his side was pierced!

Joseph did not know what was in store. If he had, he couldn't have changed it. The scriptures had to be fulfilled and nothing in heaven or on earth could stop it from happening. At least he now understood more in a few minutes that he had most of his life. Yet he did not know the full meaning of what this really meant, not only for him, but also for the world.

Chapter 6

The Day that Time stood Still!

The day of the dedication of the third temple has finally arrived. Every news organization in the world is on hand to witness the historic event. Schools have dismissed for the day. Work has stopped as the entire world is glued to a television screen to see this momentous occasion. Chancellor Romulus has brought world peace. He has stopped the economic catastrophe that was sure to happen. There is worldwide happiness for the first time in history.

Nearly everyone loves him. Especially the people of Israel for single handedly being responsible for them having the third temple. It is only fitting that he presides over its dedication. He also wanted the Pope there to share in the glory. After all, the Pope had also brought people together from around the world to contribute to its construction.

At 8:00 A.M. Central Stand Time in America, people are glued to their television screens and every communication device in existence. In Jerusalem, it is several hours later at exactly 3: P.M. in the afternoon.

Outside, in front of the new temple, news reporters are standing, while international dignitaries are seated. It is the same spot where Chancellor Romulus gave the announcement of finding the Ark. Cameras are trained on the front of the temple and billions of people from around the world are watching in anticipation of getting their first look at the inside of the new temple. They had heard rumors that it was beyond belief. The walls were reportedly lined with pure gold and the best wood on earth. The bowls and cups the priests were to use were said to be made of solid gold. Tables were also overlaid with gold and silver. One of the grandest sights was a giant solid gold menorah, weighing in at one hundred and twenty pounds, which stood just inside the giant front doors.

At five minutes before the hour, a long black limousine pulls up in front of the temple with several other cars following behind it. As soon as the cars stop, the doors open and several bodyguards jump out and rush to the limousine. After opening the doors on the limousine, they stand to the side as Chancellor Romulus, the Pope and Prime Minister Shalom step out and walk to their seats behind a podium that is in front of the temple and the crowd.

Prime Minister Shalom first steps to the podium. A hush comes over the crowd and all that can be heard are the clicks of the cameras.

"Ladies and gentlemen, friends, neighbors, dignitaries and honored guests. It is my great pleasure and honor to be standing here today. A day that my people have hoped for, have longed for, but never knew would be possible in our lifetime. For centuries, we had little hope that this day would come. But today our faith is renewed. Our hopes are high. And it is because of one man—a man of vision, of strength and of peace."

The prime minister pauses and looks to his side at the pope and the chancellor then back at the crowd. "My speech will be brief because the entire world is waiting for the man that has made this day possible. I will now step down and let another man that has also made this day possible, Pope Peter, say a few words."

With that, the prime minister leaves the podium and the pope comes and stands to make his speech.

There is applause as Pope Peter holds up his hand in a gesture of thanks. A few seconds later, the applause dies down and he begins.

"Good afternoon ladies and gentlemen, the faithful and those that need the faith. It is an honor to be with such a man as Chancellor Romulus. As said, he is a man of vision, great vison. He is a man rich in wisdom and a man the world has been waiting for, for a very long time. He has come at this time in history as an instrument of God. He has brought peace to our world by his strength and his wisdom. He has accomplished what no other has been able to do. This shows that God is with him. Let there be no doubt of that fact. As I am in the office of Saint Peter, and by the virtue and righteousness of God himself, have been given the right to declare what is holy. I declare that this man has been placed in our midst for one purpose. That purpose is to lead the world to a better place. It may take time, but if we will follow, he will lead us to a glory of which we have only dreamed. Now I want to introduce once again the man that has made this day possible, Chancellor Nicolas Romero Romulus."

Everyone stands and applauds as the pope takes his seat and the chancellor steps to the podium.

The applause lasts for two minutes as he waits to speak. Finally, the people once again take their seats. Looking over the large crowd of dignitaries from around the world and the hundreds of news reporters that have come to record this occasion, he begins.

"Thank you, one and all, for this stupendous turn out. I have been waiting for this moment a very long time," he said, with a wide smile. "I will not say but a few words because I know everyone wants to see the inside of the temple. As you can see, the outside is glorious. The inside is much greater. Before we go inside, I would like to thank Pope Peter for the kind and gracious words he spoke. Likewise, I wish to thank Prime Minister David Shalom. Most of all, I would like to thank the people of the world for having the faith in me. Without that faith and trust, I could not have built this grand temple.

I will not waste any more time because I know you are all anxious to see the inside of the temple. I know you will be astounded as will the world. I also have a surprise inside that I believe will very much astound and astonish you. Therefore, let us go into the Temple."

At this time, Chancellor Romulus, the pope and Prime Minister Shalom lead the foreign dignitaries and news people inside.

Among the first to come inside is Joseph Aaron, the High Priest. Several news reporters, along with their camera crews, follow him. Other news reporters and camera crews have run up front to get video of the chancellor as he and the others come inside.

As the people come through the doors, it is immediately evident that they are awestruck. Everyone is looking around not knowing what to look at next for the beauty is astounding. The afternoon sun is coming through the many stained-glass windows high overhead and shining on the walls of gold. The walls glow and diffuse the light all through the temple. The giant gold menorah has seven candles lighting the entrance, which also helps make the gold and silver shine.

As the chancellor and the ones near him walk towards the back of the temple, they come to the Holy of Holies.

The Holy of Holies is housed in a separate room. It is like a building within a building. The height of the new temple is a hundred feet to the celling, four hundred feet long and two hundred feet wide. It has two dozen giant, eight-foot thick pillars made of marble. They are inlaid with gold inside to support the great weight of the temple. The special building for the Holy of Holies sits in the center towards the back. It has its own walls and ceiling. It is sixty feet long by forty feet wide and a little over thirty feet high.

As the chancellor waits for everyone to come near, he stands next to the huge, royal blue curtain that hides the most precious artifact in the world— the Ark of the Covent.

The magnificent temple is there to house and protect the Ark. Inside the Ark are the tablets of stone with the Ten Commandments, which were written by the finger of God. There is also an earthen jar. Inside the jar is some manna that came from heaven that fed the Israelites when they were in the desert for forty years. Then there is Aaron's rod that budded when he was chosen to be the first High Priest.

The blue curtain that hides the Ark is huge. It goes all the way from near the celling, which is about thirty feet high. It also goes across the special room that is forty feet wide. The curtain is also four inches thick and weighs nearly three tons.

As the camera crews gather around the chancellor, he stands with a smile. When they are all in place, he reaches up and lays his hand on a button that opens and closes the great curtain. "Ladies and gentlemen, I want you and the world to see what I have built," and with that he pushes the button and the curtain begins rolling back.

As the curtain comes back, there are gasps as everyone sees the inside of the room and the beautiful Ark. The Holy of Holies is even more magnificent than the rest of the temple, if that were possible. The walls are covered in gold and silver. Intricate designs of angels, fig leaves, pomegranates, and doves are carved on every wall and ceiling. The Ark sits on a gold platform with silver trim. The platform stands two feet high. The legs are elaborately carved with olive leaves above and at the base is the head of a lion with its mouth open as if it is roaring.

Beside the ark and to the right is a huge throne. It, too, is made of gold and silver with a bright red velvet seat and back. The gold arms and back also have olive leaves carved on them and the ends of the arms have the same lion heads as the feet of the table that supports the Ark.

Beside the throne is a small silver table with a golden cup sitting on it with all manner of jewels on the outside. Beside the cup is a golden crown with the same kind of jewels, such as rubies, emeralds, diamonds, opals, topaz and many others.

Then to everyone's surprise, beside the table stands a life-size image of Chancellor Romulus. It appears to be a golden statue but looks more like a wax figure. It looks so real, it almost looks alive.

The pope then walks up to the Ark and stands beside the Mercy seat. Chancellor Romulus walks up beside the pope and kneels before him. The pope says some words no one can make out and the chancellor rises to his feet. The pope steps to the side so that Chancellor Romulus is standing facing the Mercy Seat.

The pope then turns to those that are gathered before him and says, "This man is the god of this temple!"

With that, the Chancellor puts forth his arm, takes out a small knife, makes a cut across his wrist and lets his blood pour onto the Mercy Seat. The clock in Jerusalem says 3:35 P.M.—back at Rob and Janet's home, the clock has just stopped at 8:35 A.M.!

No one knows what to say or think, but the cameras catch everything. Joseph is sickened by what he has just witnessed, but it is not over yet. A moment later, the pope hands Chancellor Romulus a cloth and holds it on his wrist as he walks to the throne. Taking a seat, he looks at the crowd as the pope walks over, picks up the golden crown that is on the table beside the throne and places it on his head.

"I crown you the Rex Romulus Maximus", (which means the Ultimate King Romulus).

The Chancellor looks at those gathered as Pope Peter smiles and steps to the side.

"I am Rex Maximus! I am King! I am the King of all Kings! I am God Almighty!" he shouts. "You will worship me from this day forward! I have the blessing of the Pope and I have the power of God—for I am God!"

At that very moment, what everyone thought was a statue begins moving and speaking. Everyone gasps as the android says, "I am your God! You will have no other gods before me! You will worship me and no other!"

Joseph, the High Priest, is shocked beyond words, but at that moment the scripture of Daniel comes to his mind. This had happened before when Antiochus Epiphanes had desecrated the temple. He had poured pig's blood on the altar and erected a statue of Zeus in the temple, but this is far worse. The Ark was not there at that time. This time it is, and the blood that was on the Mercy Seat was the most precious blood in the universe, for it was the blood of the son of God. Sinless blood that was shed to save the world! This man had just polluted that blood by putting his own sinful and evil blood over it. It was the greatest blaspheme of God in the history of the world. It was truly an abomination above all abominations! It had to take place, however, for it has been predicted from the foundation of the world.

Chapter 7

Supper Time

Back at Rob and Janet's house, they are both in shock. Janet looks at Rob, "What does this mean, Rob?"

"I don't know, but it can't be good. It means *that man* believes he is God Almighty."

"How can he think that?"

"His power and prestige have gone to his head. He has brought peace but at what cost?"

"That still does not answer the question about the clocks stopping," Janet said. "Why did all the clocks stop at the same time?"

"I don't know. The TV works and no one has said anything about any power surge that might have affected it. We can turn on the radio and see if there is anything on it."

"That's a good idea. I'll turn it on."

Going to the kitchen counter, she flips on the radio. The radio announcer is talking about what has just happened in Jerusalem. Janet turns to every station and it is the same.

While she is doing that, Rob is changing the TV channels trying to find any information about why the cell phones won't work or why the clocks would stop. Again, the only news is what has just happened at the temple in Jerusalem.

Turning off the radio, Janet comes back into the living room to Rob, who is now sitting on the sofa. "What are they saying, honey?"

Rob looks up at her worried face. "They just said that nearly every country in the world is preparing for war."

"War!"

"Yeah. The world leaders believe that Chancellor Romulus, or Rex whatever he said he wants to be called, is going to try to take over the world."

"What are we going to do?"

"What can we do?" Rob said, as he hits the off button on the remote.

Standing to his feet, he walks to the front door and stares out the glass at the front yard. Janet walks over beside him and puts her arm around his waist.

"What is that?" Rob exclaimed.

"What's what?" Janet said, glancing up at Rob's face.

"The trees across the road look different."

"Look different? What are you talking about?"

"Yeah, the trees are huge and none of them look the same!"

Janet then looks out the window. "Oh, my Lord, Rob! Everything does look different."

"Let's go outside. I've got to see what this is."

Opening the door, they both walk out onto the front porch. As they come outside, they can scarcely believe their eyes. As they stand there, they begin looking around. In all directions, nothing looks the same. The yard looks as it always did, but beyond the mailbox, it doesn't.

"Where's the road, Rob?" exclaimed Janet.

"There is no road!"

The gravel road that ran in front of their house is no longer there. Where the road once was, it is now a forest.

Rob takes his wife's hand and leads her from the porch. They begin walking out into the yard. "I can't believe this," Rob said. "I just can't believe this."

Going to the mailbox, they both stop. "Our mailbox is still here," Janet said, "but how could giant trees be growing where the road used to be?"

"I don't know, but look behind the house."

Janet turns around and looks down the hill. "Where are the cornfields, Rob?"

"They're gone, too. Everything is gone. It's like the world around us has aged a hundred years.

Rob begins walking to the edge of the yard where the giant trees are growing. Janet is behind him as Rob reaches for one of the huge oak trees that's standing where the gravel road was the day before. As Rob's hand goes towards the tree, Janet shrieks, "Rob! Don't touch it!"

Instantly, Rob jerks back his hand. "That's unreal," he said, as he puts his hand forward again.

"Don't, Rob," Janet, said, "It's frightening me."

Each time Rob's hand leaves the yard and comes near the tree his hand disappears!

"There must be some kind of barrier," he said, turning and looking at Janet. He then put his foot out, and it, too, disappears when it gets close to the tree.

"Rob! Please, stop! I'm afraid."

"I want to see something," he said. "I want to step to the other side and see what's there."

"God, no! Don't do that! You might disappear and never come back!"

"Here," he said, "hold my hand and don't let go. I'm just going to peek on the other side to see what it looks like."

"Please don't, Rob."

"It will be all right, sweetheart. I'm not going all the way. I'm just going to stick my head on the other side and look around. I need to know what's going on."

"Be careful, Rob," Janet said, as he holds his hand very tightly.

Slowly Rob puts his face up to the invisible barrier. A second later, he puts his head through.

"Rob, stop!" Janet yells as she tries pulling him back onto her side.

"It's okay, honey," she hears him say, but his head is gone. It looks as if he is the headless horseman of storybook legend.

Seconds later, he pulls his head back, turns and smiles. "It's amazing, honey."

"What did you see?"

"Everything on that side looks like it does from here, but when I looked back towards you and the house it was gone!"

"Gone?"

"Yep. I could not see you, the rest of my body or anything. It looks just the same as it does on that side. It is just a forest."

"Please, don't ever do that again. You know your head was gone when you stuck it through to the other side, don't you?"

"I know, but it didn't hurt. Take you hand and reach for the tree."

"I don't want to."

"It's all right. Here I'll take your hand and we both can reach through the barrier."

"I'm afraid, Rob."

"Here," he said, taking her hand. "There's nothing to be afraid of," and they both reach for the tree.

As their hands come near the huge oak, they disappear as if they were reaching through an invisible black curtain, a door into another world, another time or another dimension.

Pulling their hands back, Janet smiles. "That's so strange. It didn't hurt at all."

"You would never know anything was there if you didn't see your hand disappear. But I wouldn't want to take the chance of going all the way to the other side. We might not be able to get back. Maybe if I tied a rope around my waist and you stayed on this side," Rob teased.

"Rob, don't you dare do that to me! That would scare me to death."

"I won't," he said, with a grin. "I have satisfied my curiosity. I sure don't want to press my luck. At least not until we find out what's going on."

Just then, they hear what sounds like thunder in the distance and it begins to grow dark. "Must be a storm coming," Rob said.

"I don't see a cloud in the sky," Janet replied. "It's as clear as a bell."

The noise only grows louder as they begin to see the trees in the distance sway as if a wind is blowing.

"This is strange," Rob said. "How can there be a storm with no clouds?"

"Could it be jet aircraft?"

"Maybe, but it sounds more like a wind, not a jet."

As they are speaking, there appears a dark mass over the trees behind the house. It is black and looks to be about a quarter of a mile wide. "What in the world is that?" Janet exclaimed.

"I'm not sure, but we'll know in a few seconds because it is getting closer."

The morning sun begins to dim and then grow dark. "Oh my, Lord!" Rob said. "I can't believe it."

"What are they, Rob?"

"They're birds!"

"Rob, I've never seen so many birds. There must be millions of them. What kind are they?"

"I'm not sure, but I'll soon find out," he said, as he begins walking quickly to the house. "I'll be right back." A few seconds after he enters the house, he comes back out holding his .22 rifle.

By this time, the sky is dark with tens of thousands of birds going overhead.

"It raining," Janet said, as Rob comes near.

"That's not rain," he said pointing to the ground.

Janet looks to see that it indeed is not rain, but bird droppings. The droppings are falling all around them.

"Are you going to shoot one?"

"I want to find out what they are. I have a good idea, but it's impossible," Rob said, as he puts the rifle to his shoulder and fires into the flock.

Instantly, three birds tumble from the sky, landing in the yard a few feet away.

Rob walks over, leans down and picks up the nearest one.

"What kind is it, Rob?" Janet asked as Rob turns towards her.

"You won't believe it. I don't believe it."

"What don't you believe?"

Rob holds it up for her to see as he takes a step closer. It is a passenger pigeon!"

"A pigeon? I've never seen a pigeon like that around here before. It looks almost like a mourning dove, but bigger."

"Honey, passenger pigeons have been extinct for over a hundred years! They once numbered in the billions but they were all killed in the latter part of the 1800's."

"How can it be a passenger pigeon, then?"

Rob shakes his head. "That I don't know, but I do know one thing."

"What?" Janet asked.

"The woods around us did not age a hundred years— we have gone back more than a hundred years in time, maybe more than a thousand years!"

"Went back in time?"

"Went back in time—or maybe to a different dimension. I don't know. But I do know this is a passenger pigeon and they once lived here."

Janet looks as if she is in shock.

"Let's hurry and get back in the house," Rob said, as he walks over to retrieve the other two birds. "We'll have squab for supper tonight."

Chapter 8

A Place out of Time

As Janet and Rob come in the house, the roaring outside begins to subside.

"I guess it was a small flock of pigeons this time," Rob said, as he picks up a page of newspaper to use to clean and dress the pigeons.

"Small flock," Janet remarks. "There must have been at least a hundred thousand!"

"Honey, some of the flocks took days to go by and was three hundred miles long and a mile wide."

"And they were all killed?"

"Yep. In just a few years. Men went to their nesting grounds and used burning sulfur and nets to catch and kill millions. They shipped them to fancy restaurants in St. Louis, Chicago and New York where they sold for one and two cents apiece."

Janet watches as Rob removes the skin on the pigeon's breast and slices on each side of the breastbone.

"It is dark meat," Janet said.

"Yeah, birds that migrate have more blood vessels in their breasts. That's what makes it dark. A chicken has a white breast because they do not migrate and do not have as many blood vessels. The blood vessels are necessary to supply more oxygen to the muscles for flight."

Janet smiles, "I have a very smart husband."

Going to the sink, Rob washes the breast meat. "Here ya' go, sweetheart," he said, handing them to Janet. "We will roll them in flour and fry them for supper."

"Are they good?"

"I've eaten dove and regular pigeon, so they should taste about the same. You know, only the finest restaurants serve squab."

"I've heard of squab, but I never knew for sure what it was."

"Squab is a young pigeon. We can have onions fried with the meat if you like. They're not bad that way."

"Sounds good to me," Janet, said.

After placing the meat in a small plastic bag, Janet puts them in the refrigerator. She then turns to Rob, who is standing looking out the kitchen window in deep thought.

She asks, "Rob, what is really going on?"

"Honey, you know as much about it as I do. I haven't the slightest idea of what is happening."

"Nothing seems real anymore."

"I know what you mean. It is like a dream that we can't wake from."

"I'm scared, Rob," Janet said, as she steps closer.

Turning half way around, Rob puts his arm around Janet and holds her close. "At least we're together."

Janet holds him tight. "I'm so glad of that. I don't know what I would do if you weren't with me."

After they hold one another for a minute or so, Rob looks at Janet, lifts her chin and tenderly kisses her lips. "Let's go sit down and try to figure this out, all right?"

Janet nods.

Going into the living room, they sit on the sofa beside one another. Rob puts his arm around Janet as she lays her legs across his lap.

"The way I see it," Rob said, "is that we are in a kind of bubble. All around us is a world that existed long ago. It seems that our house and the nearby property is in a place out of time. We are in one time and everything surrounding us is in another time."

"What does it mean?"

"I'm not sure, but things are beginning to make a little bit of sense. The clocks all stopped at 8:35."

Janet nods, "Yes, but what does that mean?"

"It was at that time that Chancellor Romulus claimed he was God. And did you see what he did just before that?"

"I saw him go to the Ark of the Covent and pour blood on it."

"He poured his *own* blood on it. He also had a statue of himself beside the Ark, and did you see the statue move and start talking. It must be some kind of android. But I've never seen one that looked so real. Even when it moved it seemed life-like, not at all like a robot."

"What does that have to do with the clocks stopping?"

"I don't know a lot about it, but I do know that only the High Priest could go in and put blood on the Mercy Seat. The blood also had to be from a lamb that was perfect. To do otherwise was an abomination to God. I do know that."

"But why would that make the clocks stop and hurl us back in time or whatever has happened?"

"I'm not sure, but I'm going to try and find out. I know that if he claimed to be God, that it was blasphemy and if he then put his blood, the blood of a blasphemer on the Mercy Seat, *that* might have done it."

"Yeah," Janet said. "I recall our preacher had a sermon about that not too long ago."

"I've read it myself when I was married to Karen," Rob said. "We used to study quite a bit. She was a very good, spiritual woman. She studied more than I did and I remember her talking about that too. Let's get our Bibles and see if we can find it."

Chapter 9

Time, Times and a Dividing of a Time

(It is now April 6, 2033)

Going to the bedroom, Janet returns in a minute with two Bibles. "Here's yours, honey" she said, as she hands it to Rob.

Rob takes it from her hand. "This is Karen's old study Bible," he said, as he looks up at her with a smile. "She has it all marked up when she used to study it, maybe we can find something she marked."

Both begin searching. After a couple of minutes, Rob sees a paper that Karen had placed in one of the Gospels. He opens the Bible to the Gospel of Matthew, takes out the piece of paper and begins to read. "I think I found something."

"So quickly?" Janet said.

"Yeah, Karen had a paper stuck inside that she wrote a bunch of stuff on about end time and prophecies."

"Prophecies?"

"Yeah, right here it is. She has it written down and she has it underlined in her Bible. It's in Matthew, Chapter 24, verse 15. It says, "When you shall see the abomination of desolation spoken of by Daniel the prophet, let him that reads understand."

"That must be it, Rob. What else does it say?"

"It's not good."

"What?"

"It is Christ speaking and he said there will be a time of trouble the world has never seen or will never see again."

"Isn't that what they call the Great Tribulation?"

"That's it. But there's more. It says here that unless the time is shortened no flesh will be saved."

"Does that mean the human race will totally destroy itself?"

"That's exactly what it means."

"If that's true, why are we here in this place? It doesn't make sense. It is like we are in a prison."

"No, not a prison, Janet—a refuge. We are in a safe place."

"What's going to happen next?"

"I don't know, but here is something else that Karen has marked. It's in Revelation Chapter 12. It is another prophecy."

"Chapter 12?" Janet said, as she begins searching for the scripture. "What does it say?"

"It's in verse 14 and says that the woman was given two wings of an eagle where she flies to the wilderness. It is a place that God has prepared and she is nourished and protected there for a time, times and a dividing of a time."

"What does that mean?"

"Karen has some notes here. The woman is the church and the 'times thing' she said is three and a half years or 1,260 days."

"Three and a half years?" Janet said. "We will be here for three and a half years! How will be survive? What will we eat? What about medicine? I have to have my medicine!"

Seeing that Janet is becoming overwhelmed by everything that has happened, Rob tries to calm her. "I don't know. Someone is in control and it has to be the Almighty. We just have to trust that he will provide. I have quite a bit of ammunition for my rifle and shotgun. I can hunt for some of our food."

"What about the winter?" Janet said, with worry in her voice. "We will run out of gas for the space heater. And the gas won't last too long for the stove that we have to cook on. The hot water tank also uses gas. We will not have any hot water to bathe or wash our clothes."

Rob goes over and holds her. "It will be alright, sweetheart. Somehow I know everything will be alright."

Chapter 10

A Time to Heal

It had been a very long day. So much had happened that it was difficult to wrap their minds around it. Bedtime finally arrived and both are looking forward to a good night's sleep. They don't know, however, if sleep will come.

Climbing into bed, Janet turns toward Rob and puts her arms around him. Rob turns towards her and lays his arm over her waist. As Janet lies there, she looks into her husband's eyes.

"I can't believe what has happened. It still doesn't seem real."

Rob looks into his wife's worried eyes. "I know. It feels like we are in a dream—no, a nightmare."

"Rob, I've been thinking. How are we going to make it? We can't go into town for groceries, we can't get medicine. I was going to fill my blood pressure medication in a few days. I also need my pain medication and," but she doesn't get to finish her sentence because she is interrupted by Rob.

"This is incredible!" Rob said, as he suddenly bolts up in bed.

Janet is taken by surprise and thinks something is terribly wrong. "What is it, honey?"

Rob is putting his hands over his ears and then taking one then the other off. "I can't believe it!"

"What's wrong, Rob?"

"I can hear! I can hear out of my right ear!"

"You can hear?"

"Yeah, you remember me telling you about having a hearing loss in my right ear. I haven't been able to hear out of that ear all my life. I had constant ear infections in it as a kid. I had surgery on it when I was in my thirties. But I never could hear much out of it. Now it is as good as the other one!"

"Are you sure?" she asked hardly able to believe it herself.

Rob is beaming. "Here," he said. "I'll cover my left ear with my hand and you whisper something really low and see if I can hear you."

"What do you want me to say?"

"Say anything, but whisper it very softly."

"Can you hear me?"

"I can hear you! Whisper something else, but even softer."

"I love you, honey."

"I love you, too."

"How much hearing loss did you have?"

"It was nearly sixty percent. I could not hear any low tones in it at all. This is a miracle," Rob said, with joy that Janet had never seen. "I want to check something else," he said, as he looks at her.

Rob, reaching over, brushes Janet's hair from her face. She always wore her hair over the left side of her face because of a scar she's had since she was twelve years old. She got it when she fell from a bicycle. "Your scar, honey. It's gone!"

"What? It can't be."

"Go look in the mirror. I thought there was something different about your face a minute ago when we were lying here."

Sliding out of bed, Janet goes to the dresser, pulls her hair out of the way, and looks at her left temple. "It *is* gone!" she said, as she keeps searching trying to find it. "How can that be?"

Rob notices that she is not wearing her glasses. "Can you see that the scar is gone?"

Janet turns to him, "Yes, honey, I just said I could see that it was gone."

"I mean can you see it clearly. You're not wearing your glasses."

Janet seems dazed. "Yes. Everything was very clear." She begins looking around the room. "Rob, I can see everything better than I ever could—even with my glasses on!"

"I bet your blood pressure is normal, too. I thought it was a little odd that my sinuses weren't clogged today. I can breathe better than I have since I was a kid."

"That is amazing," Janet said.

"I'm going to check something else," Rob said, as he pulls up the right leg of his pajamas.

Sitting on the edge of the bed, he brings his foot up into his lap. "The scar I had on my foot is gone, too. I've had that scar ever since I cut it in the Ohio River while I was wading, back when I was a young teenager."

"I don't understand what is happening."

"Neither do I, but it is a miracle." Then he remembers something else. "How does your back feel?"

"My back? I haven't thought about. Come to think about it, it has not bothered me all day."

"I bet it is healed, too."

Janet moves from side to side to see if her back hurts when she moves a certain way. It always has in the past, but now it doesn't.

"My back feels fine," she said, looking over at Rob.

Rob stands, takes off his pajamas and slides back under the covers. "I feel like I'm in perfect health. I feel as I did when I was eighteen-years-old."

"Eighteen?"

Rob has a big smile as he looks over at Janet who has just come back to bed. "Yep, and you know what they say about a man when he is eighteen?"

"What's that?" Janet asked with a grin.

"That's when he is at the peak of his sexual desires."

"Does that mean you want to take advantage of all that energy and those intense sexual desires?"

"Come here and I'll show you," he said, rolling across the bed, taking her in his arms and kissing her.

Chapter 11

Half Empty or Half Full?

At breakfast the next morning, Rob is sitting at the kitchen table staring out the window when he turns to Janet. "The grass is getting pretty tall. I was going to mow it today."

Janet, who is in deep thought herself, is jarred back to the present. "You were going to mow?"

"Yeah, I was waiting 'til the grass got tall enough this spring to start mowing. But now I don't know if I should or not. I only have enough gas to mow one more time. Then I guess we'll just have to let the yard go."

"That will look awful."

"I know, but there's certainly no way to get any more gasoline."

"I think you should go ahead and mow. It will do you good to get outside and do something that's normal."

"I suppose you're right," Rob said, getting up from the table.

"I'll do the dishes then come out and help you trim with the push mower," Janet said, as she began clearing the table.

"That's fine if you want."

Rob then goes outside to the shed to his riding mower. As he comes inside, he walks over and lifts the hood of his mower, pulls out the dipstick and checks the oil. He then remembers he changed the oil last fall. "I guess all I need to do is fill the tank and I'll be ready," he says to himself.

Beside the mower is a five-gallon gas can, which is about half full. Opening the gas cap on the mower, Rob picks up the can of gas and begins pouring it in the tank. "I wish I'd gotten more gas," he said, as the can empties.

It takes nearly every drop to fill the mower. Rob shakes the gas can and hears a tiny amount of gas swishing around inside. He estimates there might be perhaps four ounces left. "Janet won't be able to trim," he says to himself as he sits the can down. "There's not enough gas left to last five minutes in the push mower."

Rob had run both mowers out of gas last fall as he always does before winter. Old gasoline can become gummy and clog a carburetor if it is left too long in the engine and tank.

Getting on the mower, Rob starts the engine, puts it into gear and drives out the door. After engaging the blades, he begins the pleasant chore of mowing the lawn. As he begins across the front yard, the sun is pleasantly warm, the redbud trees are in full bloom and the dogwoods are about ready to show off their white blossoms. It feels good to be mowing again after a long cold winter.

After Rob mows about half of the front yard, he looks up and sees Janet going to the shed. He almost goes and tells her that there is no gas left, but figures she will see that the gas can is empty in a minute.

A couple of minutes later, he looks up to see Janet coming out of the shed with the push mower. "Why is she bringing the mower out for?" he thinks to himself. "She won't be able to mow but a few minutes and it will be out of gas. I guess I better go and tell her."

As he's driving his mower closer, he sees she is about to try and start it. She has never been able to start it herself and he is wondering why she is even going to try.

Before he gets there, however, she pulls on the starter rope and the mower kicks off on the first pull. "The old mower started. I can't believe she got it going herself," Rob said to himself.

Pulling up beside her, Rob disengages the blades and steps on the parking break. "Honey," he said, trying to talk over the running engines. "I used all the gas for the riding mower."

"There's plenty of gas, Rob. I could barely lift the gas can to put some in the push mower."

"There can't be. I just emptied it all into this mower."

Janet looks somewhat puzzled as Rob shuts off the engine of his mower and steps off. "There's plenty of gas, Rob. It's in that red plastic five-gallon can sitting in the shed."

"I know. That's the one I used. That's the only large gas can I have," he said, as he goes into the shed.

Janet lets go of the mower handle, which stops the engine and walks into the shed behind her husband.

Coming inside, she sees Rob go to the gas can and reach down to pick it up. As he pulls up, however, he suddenly has to struggle to lift it.

"See, it's nearly full," she said.

"It is full—all the way full," he said, with bewilderment in his voice. "It is nearly running over."

Even Janet is somewhat surprised because she used some in her mower. "Rob, it can't be all the way full because I used some in the push mower."

"It is all the way full, honey. It was empty. It was totally empty," he said, sitting it back on the floor and looking up at her.

"That can't be, can it?"

"I don't know, but it is."

"What does it mean, Rob?"

"I guess it means we will never run out of gas."

Chapter 12

The Visitors

The following morning as they are finishing breakfast, they hear a soft knock on the front door.

Looking up from his coffee, Rob looks across the table at Janet. Both have shock on their faces. "My God, who could be here?" Rob said.

Janet is facing the living room as she sits at the kitchen table and can see through the front door window. There are two figures standing on the front porch. "I don't know, Rob, but it looks like there're two men on the front porch."

Slowly Rob gets up from the table.

"Rob, maybe you should get a gun," Janet said, the worry clearly noticeable in her voice.

"No, I don't believe we should be afraid."

Going to the door, Rob opens it. Standing there are two men. Both are dressed in buckskin clothing and appear to be early American frontiersmen. One has silver hair, which is rather long, down to his shoulders, with a matching full beard. He also has a string of green and white beads around his neck, which looks as if Native Americans made it. The other man looks like a slender Grizzly Adams with dark brown hair and full beard. He is wearing a coonskin cap. Both have smiles on their faces as they look at Rob. "Good morning, Mr. Blackburn," said the one in the coonskin cap.

Rob is taken aback that they know his name, but he manages to reply, "Good morning."

"How are you on this beautiful spring morning?" the other man said.

"Do I know you gentlemen?" Rob asked.

"No," said the man in the coonskin cap. "We know you, however."

Rob is still very confused as to what is going on, when the man with the necklace asked, "How have things been going these last few days?"

"Fine, I suppose. I don't know what has happened."

"That's why we have come," the man with the cap replied. "We have come to make you understand what has happened and what is going to happen."

By this time, Janet has come up behind Rob. The two men nod and the one with the coonskin cap looks at Janet, "Good morning, Mrs. Blackburn."

"Good morning," she said, nervously.

Rob's shock is beginning to wear off and he realizes he should ask them in. "Please, come in, gentlemen."

"Thank you," said the man with the necklace.

Coming in the door, Rob points to the sofa. "Won't you have a seat?"

Janet then asked, "Would you men like a cup of coffee?"

"That would be fine," the man in the coonskin cap said, as he takes it from his head.

As Janet goes to the kitchen to pour their coffee, Rob sits down across from them in an easy chair. "You said you have come to make us understand what is going on?"

"Yes," said the man wearing the necklace.

"May I ask your names?" Rob said, as he studies the men's faces. Their eyes look unlike any he has ever seen. They are very clear and greyish blue. No wrinkles are around their eyes or even on their faces.

"Our names are not important," the man with the cap replied.

Janet returns to the living room and hands the men their coffee. "Thank you," they both say as they take the cups from her hands.

Janet steps over and sits on the arm of the chair where her husband is sitting.

The man with the coonskin cap lays it across his lap and looks first at Rob then at Janet. "We have been sent here to tell you not to worry. Both of you, along with this house and the land that surrounds it, are in a place of safety."

"A place of safety?" Janet asks.

"Yes, as long as you stay here nothing can harm you. You cannot leave and you cannot communicate with anyone on the outside. As you know, you can see what is going on in the outside world."

"What *is* going on, if I might ask?" Rob said.

The man wearing the necklace looks up from his coffee and turns to them. "This is the 'Time of Trouble' that all should be fulfilled. Everything that happens from now on, God will be in direct control. The "Evil One" that you witnessed desecrating the temple and the Ark is the one that had to come."

The second man interrupts, "Yes, he had to come first and he will continue for forty-two months. He will also persecute God's people. Only a few, such as yourselves, have been spared this greatest of tribulations."

"What about our families?" Janet asked. "Will they be okay?"

"They will have to make a choice to serve God or follow the Evil One, the Man of Sin. If they chose God, they will have eternal life. If they chose not to follow God, they will receive eternal death."

"How can we warn them if we can't communicate to anyone on the outside?"

"At this very moment, God has his Two Anointed ones preparing to warn every person on earth. They will have a forty-two months mission to make known the truth. At the end of their mission, they will be killed. They will lie in the streets of Jerusalem for three and a half days. No one will bury them and the world will rejoice over their deaths."

"Why would people want to see them dead for warning them?" Janet asked.

The man with the hat sets his cup on the coffee table in front of the sofa then looks at Janet. "People, for the most part, do not want to be told they are wrong. These two witnesses will convict those that do not love God, but have pleasure in sin. That is why most of the world will hate them and rejoice over their death. They will only lie in the street for three and a half days. But this is at the very end. Before this, much needs to happen. Keep the faith and study the scriptures. That is where you will find the answers to your questions. As things unfold, you will understand more and more. Now we must be going," he said, as they both stand to leave.

The man in the necklace hands Janet his cup and nods, "Thank you for your hospitality. You have been most gracious."

Rob gets out of his chair and stands when they stand. "May I ask a question?" he said.

"Yes," said the man wearing the necklace.

"How did you get here? And why can't you tell us your names?"

"Our names are not important and we could not tell you if we wanted. We come to you by the power of God. Go to Psalm 91. Read the book of Daniel. Then read Revelation. Seek and you shall find. Knock and it shall be opened unto you."

"We will be close by," the man said, while he is putting his coonskin cap back on.

"We are always close by," the second man adds. He then looks at both of them and said, "Psalm 34 verse 7 explains it."

Rob and Janet do not know what to think but Janet keeps saying "Psalm 34 verse 7 in her mind over and over, so she will not forget.

"We must be going now, we have nearly overstayed our time," the man wearing the necklace said.

"Yes, thank you again for your hospitality," the other man said, as they begin walking towards the front door.

Walking behind them to the door, Janet said, "Please, come back when you can."

"Yes, please come back," Rob, adds. "We have enjoyed your company. I just wish I knew your names."

"Our names are not important, but look at Hebrews 13 verse 2, and you will understand even more."

Rob and Janet stand at the opened front door and watch as the two men go down the porch steps and walk across the front yard towards their mailbox. As they enter the woods, where the road once was, they both vanished before their eyes.

"That was incredible!" Rob said.

"You can say that again," declared Janet.

Rob closes the door and turns to his wife. "Let's look up those scriptures and see what they meant."

Going to the coffee table, Rob picks up Karen's old Bible. Soon he finds Psalm 34. Looking down the page to verse seven, he reads it and then looks up at Janet.

"What does it say, Rob?"

Rob holds up the Bible so she can see and Janet reads it aloud, "The angel of the Lord encamps round about those that fear him."

"My Lord, Rob. They must have been angels."

"Let's look up the other verse they said. What was it?"

"Hebrews 13:2," Janet answered.

A minute later, Rob has found it. "Here it is. It says, 'Be not forgetful to entertain strangers: for thereby some have entertained angels unawares.'"

"They were angels, honey! We had angels of God in our house!" Then Janet remembers the men told them about another scripture. "What was that first scripture they told us to read?"

"Psalm something," Rob said. "I think it was Psalm 91." A minute later, he has found it. "Here it is. It says, 'A thousand shall fall at your side, and ten thousand at your right hand; but it shall not come near you. Only with your eyes, will you look and see the reward of the wicked. Because you have made the Lord, which is my refuge, even the Most High, your habitation. There shall no evil befall you, neither shall any plague come near your house. For God shall give his angels charge over you, to keep you in all your ways.'"

Chapter 13

A Question Answered

After the visitors left and they know whom they are, Rob and Janet sit down to try to understand what is really going on.

"I'm beginning, I think, to understand what is happening," Rob said.

"What is it?" Janet asked as she looks at her husband holding Karen's Bible.

"You remember me telling you how Karen used to study her Bible?"

"Yes."

"I believe she was close enough to God that her prayers were heard."

"Her prayers?"

"Yeah. She used to tell me that she prayed for both of us and one of the prayers was that I would be kept safe if something ever happened to her. I think she felt in her spirit that this day was coming. One of the last things she told me before she died was that she loved me and God would watch over me."

"She said that when she was dying?"

"Yes, she did. When she had the heart attack, I called the ambulance but she knew it was too late. She knew she was dying. In fact, she said she didn't want to die and leave me. I told her that I knew she didn't. Then that must have been when she realized it was her time to go. That's when she looked up into my eyes and said, 'Don't worry, God will watch over you. You know that I love you.' I nodded with tears in my eyes. She then closed her eyes and took her last breath."

Rob has tears flowing down his face as Janet takes his hand. "So, you think that is why all this has happened to us?"

"I do. I think that because God honored her faith, her prayer was heard. And not only has God protected me, he has protected you. He must have known Karen was going to die. I believe he had you to come in my life, so you, too, would be safe. He judges the heart, and I know you have a good heart. I'm sure there are also many others just like us."

"How can thousands or even millions of people just disappear and no one will miss them?"

"It happened Wednesday morning at 8:35. That was right when Chancellor Romulus did what he did at the new temple. The whole world is now in chaos. People are fleeing everywhere. I'm sure many are rushing to the wilderness trying to escape what's coming. Everyone is looking out for themselves. They could not care less if a friend or even relative is missing. They will just assume they have fled somewhere that they think is safer."

"That's amazing. In the chaos, God is leading his people to safety."

"Yep, people are blinded by fear and they are not aware of what is happening right around them. It happened when God was going to destroy Sodom and Gomorrah. He blinded the people of the cities, so Lot and his family could walk out safely."

"I remember hearing that in Bible Study." Janet said.

"That has to be why God has protected us. I know I'm not worthy. But Karen was. And since husbands and wives are one in God's eyes, when she prayed, God has honored that prayer."

"I'm so glad," Janet said, "for you and for Karen."

Chapter 14

The Beauty of the Wild

The following morning, Janet is up early in the kitchen preparing breakfast.

Rob is just coming into the living room and turning on the TV.

"Rob, what kind of birds are these at the feeder? They look like parrots."

"Parrots?"

"Yeah, they are green and some have red and yellow on their head. There must be twenty or thirty at the feeder eating sunflower seeds."

Rubbing the sleep from his eyes, Rob walks to the kitchen window and looks out. It takes him a few seconds to focus his eyes. "Oh, my Lord, I don't believe it!"

"What are they, honey?"

"They are Carolina parakeets!"

"Are they rare? I've never seen any that look like that?"

"Honey, they've been extinct as long as the passenger pigeons!"

"Extinct?"

"Yes. They were once very common here, but they were all killed."

"Why would people want to kill something as beautiful as they are?"

"Mostly for their feathers. Some were captured for pets because they tamed down in just a few days. And some were killed because they liked to feed on fruit in people's orchards."

"They sure are pretty."

"They're gorgeous." Just then, Rob sees something else. "Jan, honey, come here!"

"What is it, Rob?" she asked as she sits down her mixing bowl and comes to the window.

"Look at what is going through the woods just past our mail box."

"Are those deer?"

"No, honey, they're elk."

"Elk?"

"Elk have been gone from around here even before the parakeets disappeared. The woods must have everything that once lived here two or three hundred years ago. There must be black bears, mountain lions and wolves, too."

"That sounds frightening."

"I'm not frightened. My guess would be that since we are in a place of safety, they would not harm us. I'm sorry I killed the passenger pigeons now."

"You didn't know even what they were for certain."

"I had a good idea. At least I didn't use my shotgun. If I had, I would've killed two or three dozen with one shot. That's why I used the rifle instead."

As Janet goes to the refrigerator to get some eggs, she opens the door, turns and looks at Rob. "Rob, honey, come here."

"What is it, sweetheart," he said, as he watches the elk disappear into the dark forest.

"I want to show you something."

Coming over to her side, he asked, "What is it?"

"I used four eggs yesterday and I only had six left. Now there are ten! The chickens aren't laying yet, are they?"

"No, honey, they're way too young. It will be late this summer before they are old enough to lay. They were just feathered out a month ago. They have to be about six months old to start laying."

"I thought so," Janet said, as she checks the gallon of milk. "Honey, the milk jug is full, too."

"How full was it yesterday?"

"I used it for gravy and in some potatoes so it was at least half empty."

"I'd say everything will be that way, the milk, the eggs, the flour, the gasoline and the propane. Everything we need is renewed daily."

"This is unbelievable," she said, turning to Rob and hugging him. "I was so worried, but not anymore."

"Yes," Rob said, "we are the lucky ones."

"Do you want beef sausage again with your eggs or do you want bacon?" Janet asked.

"Do we have any turkey bacon?"

"We've got both. I just took a package of bacon out of the freezer yesterday and let it thaw. I took it out with a package of pork chops I had up there."

"I think I'll have the regular bacon this morning."

Stepping over to the refrigerator again, Janet takes it out and lays it on the counter next to the stove.

"What's that smell?" Rob said.

"I don't know," Janet replied.

Rob looks up from his coffee cup he'd been sipping on and sees the package of bacon on the counter. "I didn't smell it until you took the bacon out of the refrigerator."

Janet picks up the bacon and looks at it. "That's strange."

"What?"

"The bacon has mold all over it."

"How can that be? You just took it out of the freezer yesterday, didn't you?"

"Yes. It was frozen solid just like the pork chops."

Getting up from his chair, Rob comes over to see for himself. Picking up the package, he looks at it. "It is, honey. It's spoiled."

"How can that be?"

"I don't know?" he said, going over to the refrigerator and opening the freezer. "Everything is frozen solid," he said, feeling inside. "Even the ice cream feels frozen."

"I just had a bite of it yesterday and it was fine."

"What about the pork chops you took out with the bacon?"

"I don't know. They were frozen solid just like the bacon."

Opening the refrigerator door, he looks inside. "Where are they?"

"On the bottom shelf. I put them there so they could defrost."

"Here they are." Taking them out, Rob looks at the package. "These are spoiled, too. And they stink to high heaven."

"I can smell them from here," Janet said, wrinkling her nose and making a face.

"I'll go and throw them outside," Rob said. "Maybe the possums will eat them."

After taking them to the edge of the yard, Rob dumps them in the weeds near the woods. This is the way they get rid of unwanted food. They have natural garbage disposals with the opossums and raccoons that come each night.

Coming back in the house, Rob tosses the plastic wrapping in the trashcan they have for paper. Then going to the sink, he begins washing his hands to get the smell off them. "I'm going to have to burn the wrapping that was on those packages," he said. "They'll be stinking up the kitchen if I don't."

"Why would the bacon and pork chops spoil when nothing else did, Rob?"

"I don't know, but I'm sure there's an answer."

"I certainly hope so." Janet said.

Chapter 15

A Stitch in Time

The flowing day, Janet decides she should wash the clothes. Rob's favorite shirt is dirty and he has been asking for it.

Going to the laundry room, Janet empties the clothes in the washer, dumps some detergent in and turns it on. An hour later, the washer kicks off, she goes to take the clothes out of the washer and to hang them on the clothesline outside.

Rob, seeing Janet go to the laundry room, asked, "Do you want me to help you hang out the cloths, sweetheart?"

"If you want," she replied, as she is removing the clothes and putting them in a laundry basket.

Coming into the room, Rob picks up the laundry basket and carries it outside to the line.

When reaching the line, they both begin taking out the clothes and begin hanging them. As Rob is taking out a shirt, he sees his favorite one underneath. Reaching down, he pulls it out to hang it up. When he brings it out, however, he notices that it looks brighter than it did. "Honey, did you wash my shirt in a new detergent? It looks a lot brighter."

"No, I used the same detergent as I always do."

Lifting it up, he looks for the spot near the collar that had a small hole in it. "Where's that hole?" he thinks to himself. He then looks at the front where there was a stain. He had spilled pizza sauce on it serval months earlier, but he doesn't see any stains. Then looking over at Janet he smiles, "Honey, did you buy me a new shirt just like the old one?"

"No. I could never find another one. I've looked several times."

Taking it over to her, he holds it up, "Look at this. It looks brand new. The little hole that used to be right here near the collar is not there! And the pizza stain is gone, too!"

Janet looks surprised as she looks closely at the collar. She remembered where the hole was. She also remembered trying her best to get out the stain. She even thought of suggesting that Rob throw it away but she didn't, knowing how much he liked the shirt. "It does look new. I guess we shouldn't be surprised about anything anymore. Every one of our needs is being supplied."

Chapter 16

Peace in the Valley

The next day, Rob and Janet decide to take a walk on one of the trails that Rob has made on their property. Rob has cleared a five to six-foot-wide trail all the way around and through the property, so they can take walks and see the forest. There is nearly a mile of trails and Rob keeps them mowed and even has a few benches along the way so they can stop and rest.

On this particular day, they are about a hundred yards from their house when Janet looks up and sees two small, black bear cubs coming towards them.

"Look, honey," Jan said. "Aren't those baby bears?"

Rob was looking into the trees at that very moment at a squirrel when he hears Janet say bears. "Bears! Where?"

"Right in front of us. They're running towards us."

Rob looks down the trail and sees that the two cubs are only a few yards away and are still coming towards them. "We better get back to the house; their mother is probably close by."

Turning around they start back towards the house when suddenly a huge black bear appears on the trail in front of them. Now they are between the cubs and what must be their mother. "This is not good," Rob whispers. "I wish I had brought my revolver along."

All they have for protection are their walking sticks.

Rob and Janet's hearts are pounding as the enormous bear comes closer. At the same time, Rob feels something bump his left leg. Glancing down, he sees one of the cubs. It has stopped at his feet and is looking up at him.

Janet then feels something touch her foot, and it, too, is one of the cubs. It then begins trying to climb her leg.

There is nowhere to run and Rob puts his stick in front of him. That is the only thing between him and the mother bear. "Don't move, honey," he whispers. "Maybe if we don't move, the bear will know we mean no harm to her cubs."

Janet is too frightened even to speak as the giant bear walks closer. The cub on her leg looks over and seeing its mother, makes a soft growl. The one at Rob's feet does the same. A couple of seconds later, the mother bear is within six feet of Rob and Janet when it stops and looks up at them. Then looking down at the cubs she makes a low grunt and the cubs run to her. Once they are by her side, she continues coming closer until she comes to Rob's left leg. She then pauses, glances up at him and then continues on her way down the trail. As she passes him, her side brushes up against Rob's left thigh. Rob and Janet both turn to watch her going down the trail with her cubs following close behind.

As soon as the bears are out of sight, they both sigh.

"Rob," Janet said, in a soft tone. "I was scared to death the mother would attack us."

"You're not the only one. In any normal situation, she would have. You can't get between a mother and her cubs."

"She didn't act at all upset that we were here."

"No. I would guess that all the animals are that way."

"Do you think it is like what it says in the Bible about wild animals being led by a child?"

"Yep, and the lion will lay down with the lamb."

After their nerves calm down they go back to the cabin.

Chapter 17

Where the Buffalo Roam

(It is now April 12, 2033)

The following day, as Rob and Janet were going to the garden to check on how their tomato plants were growing, they were soon to be in for another surprise. No sooner had they come out onto the front porch than they heard a rumbling. Rob, looking up at the sky said, "Sounds like thunder."

Janet looks up, too. "I don't see any clouds." Then remembering the passenger pigeons asked, "Could it be more pigeons coming?"

"No, I don't think so. They should have already migrated north by now."

As they stand there, the rumbling grows louder and the ground begins to tremble. Rob steps off the porch and walks out front so he can see in all directions.

Janet stays on the porch and stands watching Rob. As Rob takes a few more steps so he can see behind the house, she sees surprise come across his face as the ground begins shaking even more and the noise becomes almost deafening. Rob unexpectedly comes running towards the porch.

"What is it, Rob?" Janet asked as he runs onto the porch and stops beside her.

"You'll see in a second."

As Janet looks to her right, there appears a mass of dark brown shaggy beasts running at full gallop. "That's buffalo!"

"Yep, a big herd of them," Rob said, as they thunder past.

For ten minutes, the heard runs through their yard between the house and the garden. Finally, the last of the stragglers comes through with a few very young calves following close behind. The noise then subsides and they are gone back into the forest.

"Well, I guess our garden is destroyed," Janet said. "I know our lawn is a mess."

The thousands of hooves that just ran across the soft earth have churned up the grass and sod making that side of the yard look like a cow pasture. Buffalo chips are also everywhere.

"At least we have some good fertilizer," Rob chuckled.

"That was a sight I will never forget," Janet said. Then turning to Rob, she asked, "Did buffalo used to be here, too?"

"Honey, there once was maybe sixty million across the entire United States. The state of Indiana has on its state seal a picture of a bison fleeing as the forest is being cleared. Most were gone east of the Mississippi River by 1820."

"That must mean we are surrounded by what was here even before that."

"It seems so."

"We have lost so much," Janet said.

"Yes, we have." Rob then looks towards the garden. Let's go see if anything is spared in the garden."

As they come near, they see fewer and fewer buffalo tracts. When they reach the garden, they can see that the tracts go around the garden and not one animal went through it.

Chapter 18

The Blossoms

Standing there looking at the untouched garden, both are amazed that even the wild animals are guided by an unseen hand. They know, however, whose hand it is.

"Looks like everything is fine," Janet said.

"Yep, I guess we'll have some tomatoes and potatoes after all."

They then decide to go back to the house and sit on the porch swing and enjoy the morning.

On the way to the porch, Rob notices that the little apple tree he planted just a couple of weeks earlier looks as if it has some blossoms on it. "Look, honey, the apple tree is blooming."

Walking over to it, they are surprised to see that it is full of pink blossoms. "It looks pretty, Rob, but isn't it awful little to be blooming?"

"Yeah, I don't remember seeing any buds on it that looked like blossoms when I bought it. It's too little, I would think, to have that many blossoms. Maybe a hand full, but it is covered."

"They look like a tiny rose."

"They should. An apple tree is in the rose family."

"I didn't know that." Janet puts her nose to one to see how it smells. "It smells like a rose," she said, looking up at Rob. "What kind of apple tree did you say it is?"

"It is a grafted one with three kinds of apples on it. It is supposed to have Jonagold, Golden Delicious, and Honeycrisp on it. Those are my favorite ones."

"I love Honeycrisp apples.

Glancing over to the two peach trees, which are about thirty feet away, Rob notices they, too, have blossoms all over them. "The peach trees are in bloom, too. Let's go look at them."

Going over to the little peach trees, they see that they are covered in tiny pink blossoms. "Maybe we'll have some peaches this year, too," Janet said.

"It's possible. I'm amazed that they would have so many blooms at such a young age."

"Are they dwarf trees, Rob?"

"No, they're semi-dwarf just like the apple tree is, but they're still too small, I would think, for so many blossoms."

"What about the nut trees?" Janet asked. "Do you think they will bear this year?"

"No, it takes nut trees several years to bear. I just planted them two years ago, and they were 'bare root' trees when I got them. These fruit trees came in a large container with lots of roots and dirt around them."

"Let's go look anyway, okay?"

As they are walking to the backyard, they happen to look up to see a flock of very large white birds flying overhead. "Look at those, honey," Rob said, pointing in the sky. "You know what they are?"

"No, I'm not sure. Are they geese?"

"No, they're whooping cranes. They fly in formation like geese. There must be fifty or sixty in the flock."

"They look very graceful."

"They're the tallest bird in North America. When I was young, there were no more than fifty or sixty in the entire world."

After they watch the birds go by, they continue walking to the nearest pecan tree. As they approach, Janet does not see any blossoms. "They are not blooming. I thought they might if the other trees were."

Rob chuckles slightly. "Honey, nut trees don't have blossoms like fruit trees."

Janet looks at him and smiles. "Well, I don't know. What kind of things do they have?"

Nearing the tree, Rob puts out his hand and touches a long green fuzzy looking thing. "Here is a blossom."

"*That* is a blossom? It looks almost like a small green caterpillar."

"It's called a catkin. That's the blossom and if it gets fertilized a nut will grow there. The tree is just too small to be blooming. It's not over three feet tall."

"Maybe it likes the soil here."

"Maybe," Rob said. "Just because it blooms does not mean it will have nuts this fall though. Often the first couple of years a nut tree blooms it does not bear. It is a grafted tree, so I guess I shouldn't be surprised that it has a few blossoms."

"What do you mean by being a grafted tree?"

"The people at the nursery take a limb or bud from a tree that bears a certain variety of fruit or nut and grafts' or attaches' it on the root part of another tree. This way when the new branch or bud grows into a mature tree, it will produce exactly the kind of fruit or nut that the limb or bud came from."

"Can you put a limb from a peach tree on an apple tree?"

"Sure, you can, but it will die. The trees have to be closely related, sweetheart. You can put a peach and plumb together to get a nectarine. You can put a pecan limb on a hickory tree and get a hick-con."

"That sounds interesting, Mr. Teacher." Janet said, with a grin. Janet is always impressed with the knowledge her husband has. She would have known he was a teacher without him even telling her. He was always pointing out interesting things about nature and telling her as if she was one of his students.

Rob grins. "Yep, nature is something else. I love to see things grow."

"I'm sure glad the buffalo didn't tromp down our little trees," Janet said, taking her husband's hand.

Turning around, the couple starts walking back to the house and Rob looks down into Janet's eyes. "I don't think we will have to worry about any real damage from the wildlife around us. I think they know what they are to do or not to do."

Janet nods.

Chapter 19

A Time of War

As the days go by, Rob and Janet are still troubled because of what is going on in the outside world. Each night they watch the news on television and see the trouble all over the world. There are riots and terrorist acts that are killing hundreds a day. Food shortages are already being reported in places where conflicts have erupted. The New Roman Empire has declared war on several countries and is preparing to invade them. The countries that Russia took back from the European Union are being fought over.

The new self-proclaimed world king is determined that the world will buckle under his authority. He has issued a decree that every person must have an international number. Otherwise, they cannot buy or sell anything. This even means any country that does not comply will not be able to buy, sell or trade with the New Empire.

He has several arguments for the individual having this number. One is that if everyone has a personal number, no one can steal it. This way there will be no identity theft. Without money, there will be no theft of any kind. No cheating on taxes, no purchases of illegal drugs or anything he thinks should be outlawed. He has made this international number mandatory and everyone must comply within sixty days in every country on earth. If those in his country or those in his control do not receive it they will be labeled a criminal and subject to imprisonment or death. The number will be invisible and must be placed on the hand or forehead so it can be scanned. Every transaction will be recorded. The number is also tied in to a super computer that has every bit of information about every person on earth: their name, health records, criminal record, education and work history, as well as where they live or have lived. No one can get around the surety built into this system. No terrorist can infiltrate another country because they would be caught immediately. No one can buy a gun or even buy material to build a bomb without a red flag going up.

All private weapons such as guns, crossbows, bow and arrows, swords and even knives with blades longer than eight inches are now illegal. All rifles and shotguns have already been confiscated in his country and those he controls. The people have thirty days to destroy or bring in anything he deems a weapon or suffer the consequences. Anyone committing a serious crime will also be executed within thirty days.

Rob and Jan are disturbed by what they see and they do not know how bad it will get before it is over. Day after day, they watch world events, read the Bible and search for answers as to what is coming.

Chapter 20

The Visitors Return

On the morning of the first day of June, Rob and Janet are on the front porch having their second cup of coffee as usual.

Janet is looking past the mailbox where the road once was when she sees something move in the trees.

Rob is busy reading Karen's Bible that he has brought out with him.

"Rob, what are those strange birds in the trees just past the mailbox?"

Looking up, Rob sees a flash of white. As he stares into the huge oak, he sees it again, along with something large and black. "It's some kind of bird," he replied. "I'm not sure what."

As he is watching, one of them suddenly flies around the tree and lands on the side facing him and Janet. "There it is," Janet said. No sooner had she spoken then a second one flew right beside the first.

Rob stood to his feet is disbelief. The first bird was slightly larger than a crow. It had a rather long neck with a large red crest. Its back was mostly white with some black. The second bird was the other's mate. She was all black with a black crest.

"What are they, Rob?"

"They're woodpeckers. They are ivory-billed woodpeckers!"

"I don't remember seeing those around here before."

"They've been gone for many years, too. No one was even sure they lived this far north, but here they are! I never would have guessed that I'd see an ivory-billed woodpecker. They are gorgeous."

"They are beautiful. What happened to them?"

"They were killed because they were so beautiful. The vast forests they depended on were cut down and there never were very many anyway. Then, when they become rare, more were killed just so people could have a specimen to mount."

Just then, the magnificent woodpeckers both made a sound, which sounded more like a small nuthatch and took off, heading back into the dark forest. That's when Rob sees some other movement beside the oak tree where the woodpeckers have just left. "Look who's coming," Rob said, as Janet looks to see the two visitors that had come before. They were walking out of the forest near the mailbox and coming towards the house.

As they near the house, both have smiles on their faces. They are dressed the same as they were the first time, except the one is not wearing the coonskin cap. "Hello," said the one wearing the beaded necklace.

"Good morning," Janet said.

Rob stands to his feet as they come close to the porch. "Good morning, gentlemen. Welcome."

Stepping onto the porch, they shake hands with Rob. "Let me go in the house and get a couple of chairs."

"No, thank you. We won't be staying long."

"Would you like a cup of coffee?" Janet asked. "I think there's still some left from breakfast."

"Coffee would be fine. Thank you, Janet," said the dark-haired man.

Janet gets up and goes in the house as the two men lean against the porch posts. "How have things been going?" asked the one wearing the necklace.

"Everything is fantastic," Rob said, with a big grin. "Did you see the ivory-billed woodpeckers as you were coming out of the forest?"

"Yes, we did," said the silver haired man. "They are one of God's favorited creations."

The dark-haired man looks at Rob. "So, you've been doing well since we saw you last?"

"I can't believe what's happening. Just two months ago, a herd of bison came running through the yard and not one stepped in our garden. Just before that, we met a mother bear and her cubs and the mother bear walked right by us."

"Yes," the dark-haired man said, "the animals know that you are protected here. They will not harm you."

Then Rob remembers the passenger pigeons. "The first day that this happened, I saw a flock of passenger pigeons flying over and I wasn't sure what they were so I shot three of them. I didn't waste them, we had them for supper that night. If I knew everything was protected I would not have killed them."

"You are forgiven. Death has not yet been done away with. The pigeons would have died in the future. Someday, however, death will no longer be an enemy."

As they are speaking, Janet comes out with the coffee. "Here you are," she said, handing them the steaming cups.

Both nod as they take the cups from her hands. "Thank you, Janet," said the silver haired man.

"Rob, did you tell them about the gas and the eggs and stuff?"

"I'm sure they know," he replied, as he looks up at them.

They smile and the dark-haired man said, "You will never run out of anything you need as long as you are here."

"Is that why we are in perfect health?" Rob said. "I was nearly deaf in my right ear and now I can hear out of it. Janet can see without her glasses and even her back no longer hurts."

The men smile. "Have you not read that when the children of Israel came out of Egypt there was not one feeble person among them? God supplies all your needs."

Janet then remembers the bacon and pork chops spoiling. "I have a question," she said, looking at them both. "Why would bacon and pork chops spoil even though they were frozen when nothing else ever spoils?"

The silver haired man replied, "Do you remember reading what happened when God sent manna down from heaven when the children of Israel were in the wilderness?"

"I remember reading that God supplied their need every day."

"Do you remember that God told them to only pick up what they needed for each day? When some of the people disobeyed and picked up more than they needed it would spoil before they could eat it."

"I remember reading that," Rob said. "But we have taken things out of the freezer before and they never spoiled."

"Children," the dark-haired man said. "That is not why it spoiled. Have you not read what God has said?"

"What do you mean?" Janet asked.

"Go to the Bible and read God's own words," he answered. "Read what God has made holy and has set apart. Read what will happen to those that know the truth but have pleasure in disobeying his word."

"Where can we find this?" Rob asked.

"Go to Leviticus, chapter eleven," the dark-haired man said.

"And go to Isaiah, chapter 65," said the silver haired man.

"I do have a question," Rob said. "What's going to happen after all this is over?"

"You don't know?" asked the silver haired man.

"I would think there will be peace after God intervenes."

"Yes, there will be peace, and it will last a thousand years."

"But before the peace," the dark-haired man said, "will come great wrath."

"Wrath?" Janet said, looking concerned.

"Yes, soon the Wicked One's wrath will be on God's people. Then God's wrath will be on the wicked. It is all in your Bible."

"We've been reading, trying to understand," Janet said.

"We know you have," said the silver haired man. "You will understand more as time goes on. You two have been spared what most of the world is going through."

"Sad to say, it will get much worse before it gets better," the dark-haired man said. "It is a test for all those that seek the truth. It will also be punishment on all those that reject the truth."

Rob looks into both men's eyes. "We looked up the scriptures you told us about the last time we saw you. We know you are messengers from God."

"We knew you would read the scriptures. We also knew that you already knew in your heart who we were."

Rob then said, "As Janet said, we've been reading and studying every day."

"That's good. The more you read the more you will understand."

"We are beginning to understand," Janet said. "We found that our situation is much like Elijah the prophet when he stayed with the widow and her son. The meal never ran out or the oil."

"That's right," said the silver haired angel.

"May I ask a question?" Rob said.

"You may ask any question you like. We may not be allowed to answer it, but you are free to ask anything."

"I've been thinking about it a lot and I don't believe we are back in time. It seems more like we are in a different dimension. Is that true?"

"There are many dimensions. They are all around us every day. Mortal man cannot go between them, but other beings can. Someday every person will be able to go back and forth. You will also have different eyes to see many wonderful things."

"What is around us?" Rob asked. "I know we are surrounded by forests like there was long ago. But are there Indians? Is it like it was a couple hundred years ago?"

The dark-haired angels smiled. "You mean because of the clothes we wear, we look like someone that lived in America two or three hundred years ago?"

"I suppose so."

"We thought our clothing was appropriate. We had to wear something, so we chose what you might expect Americans would look like when your nation was young. Yes, you are surrounded by wilderness and it is just as it was many hundreds of years ago."

"Hundreds of years?" Rob said, his mind trying to take in what they have just revealed to him.

"It is as it was before man came and destroyed much of it," said the silver haired angel.

Rob then wanted to know something else. "We've been watching the news every day and we've seen those two men you spoke of." Rob said. "They preach hell fire and damnation. They say that unless people repent, God will destroy them. They've been listing all the sins the world is committing."

"They speak the truth. The time of grace is running out. Soon God will shut the door as he did when Noah entered the ark. It will then be too late. Many will knock, but God will not answer. God does not change. People change, but God is from everlasting to everlasting. What was a sin to him long ago is a sin now. He will condemn all liars, adulterers, thieves, murderers and those that engage in sexual perversion."

"Sir," Janet asked, "why were we spared and others were not?"

"God looks upon the heart. As your husband told you, his wife Karen had a lot to do with it. She was a Godly woman and she was very faithful. She followed Christ and not man. She was often at odds with her minister if he did not preach the truth. She kept the Sabbath, which is one of God's commandments. Her minister chose to follow his church and not God. He has not been as lucky as you have. He is being tested and severely. To whom much is given, much is required. He was in a place of authority and he knew the truth, but did not care to preach it. He loved his position in the community more than he loved pleasing God."

"Yes," the other angel said, "it was Karen's prayers that has spared you both. She had many times asked that God would protect her home and those that lived under her roof. God always honors his word and he had made a promise to himself that her household would be spared."

"It sounds like what happened when the death angel killed the first born in Egypt," Rob said.

Janet then added, "Yes, if the blood of the lamb was on the door post of the house it was spared."

"You are absolutely right. You have the invisible blood of Christ over the door post of your house," the angel said, smiling.

Rob was listening intently and he had another question. "You mentioned that I was right about my wife, Karen?"

"Yes," replied the silver haired angel.

"I only told Janet about that. How do you know what I said in private?"

"Haven't you read that every idle word that men shall speak they will give an account of it on the day of Judgement?"

This somewhat frightened Rob, for he had no idea that every word he said was being recorded.

The other angel knew what he was thinking and said. "Do not be afraid. Only the words that are spoken in anger or hate will be used against you. By your words, you will be justified and by your words, you will be condemned. No, your private words you say to your wife when you are being intimate with her are not recorded. Haven't you read that the marriage bed is undefiled?"

Rob smiles, "That's a relief."

Janet looks a little embarrassed.

The silver haired angel then looks at the other. "It is time that we should be going."

"I have another quick question," Rob said. "Are there many others like us—people that are protected?"

"There are many, but not as many as there could have been. Most did not care enough to get close to God. Now they are wishing they had. It was the same as it was in the days of Noah. The people were warned but they chose to ignore the warning. Many were warned this time, but they also chose not to listen. They will listen now and God will reap many into his kingdom because of it. God chastises those that he loves. Remember, those that truly follow God are in the world, but not of the world."

The two then set the coffee cups on a small table on the porch and go down the steps, then across the yard. Again, as they come to the woods, they fade away and disappear into thin air.

After they are gone, Rob looks at Janet. "I'll be right back. I want to know what's in the Scriptures they just told us to read."

A minute later, he comes back out with Karen's Bible and sits down in the porch swing next to his wife. "That was Deuteronomy, eleven, right?"

"Yes, I pretty sure that's what he said."

A minute or so later, he finds it and begins reading. "Here it is, Jan." After reading a couple of minutes he looked up and said, "I know why the pork spoiled."

Janet looks at him, "Why?"

"Because God said it is unclean and should not be eaten."

"That's Old Testament stuff. We don't need to do that."

Rob then turns to Isaiah. "I'm going to read the other scripture they told us about. It was Isaiah, 65.4, I believe." After he reads several paragraphs, he looks over at Janet. "Oh, my goodness," he said. "This is talking about the end of time and God's wrath on those that think they are holier than he is."

"The end of time?" Janet said, with surprise.

"Yep, it's talking about a new heaven and new earth. It also said in verse four that the wicked will be eating swine's flesh and other abominable things."

Chapter 21

A Place out of Time!

As the weeks go by, Rob and Janet begin to feel safe in their place out of time. They are witnessing things they never thought they would ever see. Now their small world is the only world.

The things happening on the outside is what seems unreal. They watch television less and less each week. The news only makes them upset. The last time they watched the news they saw people being rounded up and taken to undisclosed locations. The Chancellor or as he now calls himself, Rex Maximus, has done what he said he was going to do.

He has ordered everyone on earth to take an international number. The number begins with the New Roman Empire's name or number, which is NRE or 666. The number of the country, providence or state, then the personal number of the individual follows that number. Without this name or number, they cannot buy or sell anything.

People that have not gone along and taken the number, have been labeled criminals. Their homes have been confiscated as well as any money and given to the government. They are then beaten or thrown into prison.

Many have just been shot and left on the street as an example to others. Many women have been raped and beaten for refusing to obey the "law". Those people that do not receive the "mark," as many call it, are labeled as outcast and open season has been declared on them. It is like hell on earth and the couple does not want to think about what is happening on the outside.

They do watch a DVD of an old movie two or three times a week. Rob has a large collection of hundreds of movies. They both like about the same thing, westerns, a few action movies and science fiction. Both of them love the old Star Trek shows and movies. They feel somewhat like those on the star ship as they are in their own world and away from danger.

All their daily needs are met. The well always has good spring water flowing in it and the solar panels produce all the electricity they need. The gas can never runs out so the yard can be mowed and maintained. Working in the yard and garden or taking walks on the trails are some of their favorite pastimes. Another favorite thing to do is to sit on the front or back porch and watch wildlife come and go. Janet has been feeding the birds every day and just like the can of gasoline, the barrel of sunflower seeds and the bag of mixed seed never runs out.

As they were studying the scriptures one day, before the angels came for their second visit, they found the story about the prophet Elijah. They read how God had protected him, the widow woman and her son by the meal and oil never running out.

They also learn that Elijah's mission was three and a half years long. They did not know exactly what this meant but they felt it was parallel to what was happening to them. They knew that this terrible time of trouble was to also last three and a half years.

This was the same length of time the two witnesses were to preach a warning to the world. They also came across the scripture in Malachi 4:5, which said that God would send Elijah the prophet before the great and dreadful day of the Lord.

This was confirmed one day when they had turned on the world news. There were the two men the angels had told them about and one was claiming to be the prophet Elijah himself. He was warning people to repent because the end of the world was coming and God was about to pour out his wrath. People were terrified of him and his partner. Wherever they went and warned people there would be a drought and not one drop of rain would fall until they left. Rob and Janet had read that all during the time that Elijah had been on his mission it had not rained.

The second man said he was Enoch. Many asked him how he could be Enoch and he would not say. He said the answer is in the word of God. He also was like no man they had ever seen. He spoke with power and authority. These two men feared no one, not even Chancellor Romulus who claimed to be God. They preached against him every day. They warned people to die rather that bow down to him.

They warned people to change their ways because God's judgment was near. They pointed out all the sins the world was committing and people despised them. Many attempts were made on their lives, but anytime anyone got close enough to try to kill them a bright beam of light that appeared to be a laser would strike and kill the person. This is another reason people feared them.

Shortly after they began preaching, plagues begin to fall on those that rejected their message. Plagues of diseases, mosquitoes, lice, mice, rats, and even locusts struck the countries where they suddenly appear. Many earthquakes were reported all over the world, too. No one had ever heard of so many and often in places that had never had an earthquake before. Tens of thousands were killed because of these devastating quakes.

No one knows how these two men traveled. They would be in one country one day and the next day, they would be half way around the world in another. People began fearing these men and what was coming upon the earth because of them.

Chapter 22

The Family Comes for a Visit

Early that first June, Rob and Janet are on the front porch as they usually are after breakfast having their coffee. Rob is eating a raisin oatmeal cookie that Janet had made the day before. While they are talking about how beautiful the weather has been, Janet happens to look across the yard into the forest and sees something moving their way. She is about to tell Rob that she sees something when it comes out of the woods and into the yard. "Rob," she whispers, "there's a giant bear in the yard."

"Where?" he asked as he looks up from his cup of coffee.

"Over there, towards the garden."

"I see it." As soon as he sees it, he notices two small black cubs coming out of the forest behind the big bear. The cubs are running as full speed trying to catch up with their mother. A few seconds later, they catch up and begin walking alongside her. "They look like the ones we saw on the trail that day, honey."

"They do, don't they? Should we go in the house?" she asked looking over at her husband.

"I don't think they will hurt us."

"Are you sure?"

"We will soon find out—because here they come."

The mother bear is walking directly towards the porch with her two cubs running to keep up with her. Closer and closer they come, until they are standing at the foot of the steps. The mother bear looks to be about three to four hundred pounds and has her nose in the air as if she is sniffing something.

"I think she smells my cookie," Rob said.

Just then, the huge bear looks towards the two of them and begins coming up the steps. "Rob, it's coming on the porch," Janet whispers.

"Does the cookie smell good, old girl?" Rob said, as the bear comes up and sits down in front of him. She gets so close that she nearly steps on his toes.

Janet is sitting there beside Rob on the porch swing and the bear is so close that she can reach out and touch it.

"Here you go," Rob said as he breaks off a small piece of the cookie and hands it to her. By this time, the cubs have come onto the porch and are at Rob's feet. They also smell the cookie and begin climbing his leg wanting it. "You can have some too, little guy," Rob said, as he gives a piece to the hungry cub.

Janet is just sitting there watching the amazing sight. The second cub then climbs right onto Rob's lap wanting some of the cookie. "Here you go. Here's a bite for you, too."

By now, the cookie is gone. "Rob, do you want me to get another cookie or two."

"If you want," he replied, as the first cub begins climbing right up into his face. It then begins trying to lick his mouth because it can smell the cookie he has been eating. It is so cute that Rob has to laugh. Taking the little ball of fur in his hands, he lifts it away from his face and looks into its little black beady eyes. "Janet is going to get you another cookie. You will just have to wait 'til she comes back with it.

Janet is just now trying to get around the mother bear who is taking up much of the porch. "You will have to move a little bit," she said, as she uses her knee to gently push against the bear. When she does, the mother bear looks back and sees her trying to get by. It then moves slightly out of the way so she can pass.

A moment later, Janet comes back out with three more cookies. "I have one for each of you," she said as she hands two to Rob. "I want to feed this one," she said, reaching down on the porch and lifting the little cub up and into her arms. He begins squirming, trying to find the source of the smell of the delicious cookie. "Here it is, sweetheart," Janet said, as she begins feeding the little hungry bear from her hand.

The mother bear has been sitting there very patiently waiting for Rob to feed her. "Here you go, girl," he said, handing her the largest cookie. She quickly gobbles it down as Rob begins feeding the other cookie to the cub he is holding. Soon the cookies are gone. "They're all gone. There aren't anymore," he said, looking at the little bears curious eyes.

The mother bear seems to understand. Standing to her feet, she turns and walks to the edge of the porch, then goes down the steps and onto the ground. Turning her head to look back at the cubs, she gives a low grunt and they look towards her and want down. Janet and Rob put the cubs on the floor of the porch and they run down the steps towards their mother. On the last step, one of the cubs takes a tumble and lands on his head. The mother bear looks back and pauses a second until he gets to his feet and catches up to her. All three then head back into the forest. It will be a day that Rob and Janet will never forget.

Chapter 23

At Peace with the Beasts

After that day with the bears coming to be fed, Rob and Janet often have visitors from the forest. Elk sometimes come in the yard with their young to graze on clover. Foxes often run and play chasing one another through the lawn. They show no fear and sometimes come to the porch to look at them as they sit watching.

One day, in mid-June, a whitetail deer came with two newborn fawns. They came right near the porch and they were so darling that Janet had to go see if she could pet one. As she neared, both the fawns turn and look at her. When she reaches out her hands, they come up and smell her fingers. Reaching over she begins petting them. The mother pays little attention after she sees that her fawns are in no danger. She then continues eating some tall grass near the cabin.

The Carolina parakeets came back too. One day the feeder was empty and the parakeets were on the feeder looking to find some sunflower seeds. Janet took out a small container of seeds to give them and the parakeets did not fly away as she neared. They watched her as they perched on the feeder until she gave them some food. After that day, if they ran out of food they would fly up to Janet and Rob as they sat on the porch swing wanting them to bring out more seeds. They became so tame that they would eat from their hands.

Rob had noticed that even before the clocks stopped that some of the local animals seemed tame. An old box turtle would often come to the cabin, stop at the bottom of the stairs and watch the front door. It was a female and she was so old that the markings on her shell were faded and nearly gone. Rob estimated that she had to be over a hundred years old. He once gave her a small piece of cantaloupe and after that day, she would come back to the cabin every few weeks looking for a free handout.

Fence lizards would also lie on the porch railing sunning themselves. Rob could walk right up next to them and they would just cock their head and look at him. They seemed to know he meant them no harm. Now, however, he could actually reach down and touch them and they would pay him no mind.

Even squirrels would allow him and Janet to get very close. Rabbits would also often feed only a few feet away. They had seen this in the city, but not in the country where there were many predators and where people often hunted them.

Not long after the incidence of the bears coming and eating from their hand, Rob was reading the book of Job when he came across a scripture he could hardly believe. "Honey, listen to this," he said, looking over at Jan. "Here's what it says in Job, chapter 5. "It says, *'You will laugh at destruction and famine and need not fear the beasts of the earth. For you will have a covenant with the stones of the field and **the wild animals will be at peace with you**. You will know that your home is secure; you will take stock of your property and find nothing missing.'"*

"It says that. That's amazing!"

"Yep, that's why the animals have no fear of us."

Chapter 24

Harvest Time

As summer progressed the tomato plants were loaded with one and even two-pound tomatoes. Rob dug the potatoes in mid-July and there were about a hundred pounds in only two rows of plants.

Later that summer the peaches began getting ripe. Rob had to prop up the limbs with forked sticks to keep them from breaking. The tiny trees must have had a bushel of peaches on each one. Each day they would pick the ripe ones and have fresh fruit. The following day, they could not tell that they had picked any. Finally, all the fruit had fully ripened, so they picked all of it and put it into cardboard boxes to store in the shed. The next day, the trees were again full of fruit. They had nowhere to sore any more peaches so they left the fruit on the trees. Soon deer and bears were coming each day and eating them.

The same thing happened with the apple tree in late September. Even the wild pawpaw trees that almost never bore were full of the banana like fruits.

It was during the month of October that Rob and Janet were walking on one of their wooded trails when Rob pauses suddenly. He sees something in the path. Reaching down to the ground, he picks up a small round brown object.

It is a nut of some kind, but it has fuzzy burrs on it. "What is that, Rob?" Janet asked.

"Do you know what this is?" he said, holding it up so she can see it better.

"No, I just asked you what it was."

"I know, but you will never guess what it is."

"It's a nut, isn't it?"

"Yes, of course, but what kind?"

"It looks like a big beechnut. "

"You're close. They are related to a beechnut."

"I give up. What is it?" she said, looking at him with a big grin on his face.

"This, my dear, is an American Chestnut."

"I've never seen one before."

"Neither have I. A disease that was brought over here from Europe killed them all. They were pretty much gone by the 1930's. The disease was called chestnut blight. The wind must have blown it over here or a squirrel dropped it. The woods must be full of them. They were once as common as oaks or hickory trees before the blight hit them.

****

November came and then Thanksgiving. It was only their third Thanksgiving together since they were married and they were looking forward to it. It was a beautiful day. The weather was cool but clear and sunny. The trees had lost most of their foliage, but some of the oaks and beeches were still covered with a good many leaves. Dark red and brown leaves clung to the red oaks, while golden ones were scattered among the branches of the beech trees.

Rob and Janet rose early that morning so they could get an early start on making the dinner. They were having fresh mashed potatoes made from the ones they had dug out of their garden. Jan had a box of stuffing mix and even a can of whole cranberry sauce. They did not have a turkey, although Rob could have killed one as they were often in the yard. They had a chicken to bake that came from the freezer instead. With this, they had canned corn and Rob made a pan of golden brown, backing powder biscuits from scratch. Rob was a very good cook as he often cooked the wild game

102

he had taken. The only thing they wanted but did not have were fresh sweet potatoes. They couldn't complain, however, with most of the world starving.

About fifteen minutes before everything was ready, they hear a knock at the front door.

Surprised they look at one another. "Who in the world?" Rob said.

"Must be the two that have come before," Janet replied.

Going to the door, Rob can see two men standing on the porch.

"Is it them, Rob?" Janet asked, as she looks over at him.

"I believe so," he answered, as he opens the door. "Yes, Jan, it's our friends from the forest."

The two men on the porch smile when Rob opens the door. "Good day," said the one in the coonskin cap.

"Well, we never expected to see you two today," Rob said, with a big grin. "Won't you come in? We were just about ready to sit down for Thanksgiving dinner."

"We know," said the silver haired man, "that's why we came.

"Well, you two are welcome anytime," Rob said, as they came inside.

"It sure smells good," the dark-haired man said as he steps inside the door and removes his cap.

"We brought something for dinner," said the other man as he held up a small gunnysack.

Rob takes the sack from his hand and opens it. Inside are several large sweet potatoes.

"Thanks," Rob said. "If I would have had them a little earlier I could have fixed them for dinner."

"There's plenty of time," he replied, with a smile.

Rob seems a little surprised and has a questioning look on his face.

"Yes, you have time," he assured Rob. "Just put them in a pan—add some butter and brown sugar and they will be ready by the time the rest of the meal is done. Oh, and save one, you will need it for later."

"Okay, "Rob said. "I don't even have to peel them?"

"No, they'll be done in no time."

"You two have a seat and we'll tend to the meal," Rob said, as he heads for the kitchen.

They smile and nod. Then walk over to the sofa and take a seat.

Janet hurries and gets the brown sugar and margarine as Rob washes the potatoes at the sink, cuts them and then puts them in a pan. In less than three minutes, they are in the oven.

Janet and Rob already have the table set so Janet has only to set two more places for the guests. After she and Rob have finished setting everything, Janet goes to the oven to take out the baked chicken and biscuits. When she opens the door, she sees that the sweet potatoes are already done! "Rob," she says in a low tone, "the sweet potatoes are already brown. They're done and even the skins are gone!"

"Go ahead and take them out, sweetheart," Rob says.

A moment later, everything is on the table and ready to serve. "Men," Rob said. "Dinner is ready."

Everyone then takes their seats around the table as Janet and Rob begin serving the chicken.

After everyone has some chicken on their plates, Janet tells everyone to help themselves to whatever they want.

When everyone is finished piling their plates high, Rob turns and looks at the angels sitting at the table. He can hardly believe this is happening. "Would one of you like to bless the food?" he said.

"I would be honored," the silver haired man said. Everyone bows their heads as he begins, *"Blessed are You, O Lord our God, King of the universe, who brings forth bread from the earth. Amen."*

"Amen," everyone says.

"Is that the blessing you usually say," Janet asked.

"That is the blessing that has been said since the days the children of Israel were slaves in Egypt," he answered.

As they beginning eating their meal, Rob looks across the table and says, "It was good of you to bring sweet potatoes. For me it just doesn't seem like Thanksgiving without them."

"We were happy to have been able to contribute something for the meal."

"How did you know we didn't have sweet potatoes?" Janet asked.

"The Master knows all of your needs."

"Will you be coming for Christmas dinner, too," she asked.

The two men look at one another and then the dark-haired man says, "We do not celebrate pagan holidays."

Janet is somewhat confused. "You don't celebrate the Lord's birth?"

"We did not say that. We said we do not observe pagan holidays."

The silver haired angel then says, "You are to worship God in spirit and in truth. The truth is that our Lord was not born in December. Man has invented that day and it is a tradition of man, not of God."

"In vain do you worship me, teaching as doctrines the traditions of men," said the other man.

"Can you tell us when Christ was born?" Rob asked.

"Yes, but if he wanted you to know the day he could have easily told you."

"Is it a secret?" Janet asked.

The dark-haired angel then speaks and says, "If you keep God's Holy Days you will keep the Messiah's birthday."

"I don't understand," Janet said.

"Not many do," he replied. "God created his Holy Days for men to follow. In them, he shows his entire plan of redemption, salvation, the resurrection and his kingdom coming to earth."

"Even the Great White Throne Judgment and the New Heaven and New earth," the other one said.

"I thought those were only for the Jews," Rob said.

"My children," said the silver haired angel, "the tribe of Judah is but one tribe out of many. You are now grafted into the root. The root is the Lord himself. Our Lord was the Lamb of God that died on Passover. He was the first to be raised as the First Fruits to God. The Holy Spirit came on the Day of Pentecost. He will wake the dead when the seventh trumpet sounds on the day of Trumpets. He will gather his children to him and they will be forever at his side. He will then Tabernacle with man on earth for a thousand years."

"All of this is in the Bible?" Rob questioned.

"It most certainly is."

"We have a lot to learn," Rob said.

"That is why you are here. Keep searching and you will find."

"What you don't know will be explained someday," said the other angel. "Now we look through a dark glass and cannot see clearly, but when the Lord comes we will know as we are known."

"Why isn't it wrong to celebrate Thanksgiving?" Janet questions.

"It is never wrong to give thanks to God. We are to give him thanks in everything," the silver haired man said.

The dark-haired angel looks at his partner, then at Rob and Janet. "It is time we leave. We want to thank you for the good meal and your gracious hospitality once again."

They both smile as they look across the table at their hosts and they begin to vanish before Rob and Jan's eyes.

That was the first Thanksgiving they had at the cabin and one they will never forget.

Winter soon arrives and so does the snow. Outside it often looks like a winter wonderland. The forest surrounding them only contains mature trees. The trees are so large that Rob sometimes has difficulty identifying them. One tree that is close to their yard is a giant tulip tree. The first branches are so high that when Rob first saw it he could hardly see to tell what kind of leaves were on it. The tree must have been six or seven feet thick and nearly a hundred and fifty feet tall. The oaks were likewise huge. Under the trees, the forest floor is rather bare. This is because there is so much shade during spring and summer that it keeps small trees or bushes from growing. This means there are few plants that many animals need for food. Only when a giant tree dies or blows down in a storm, does the sun penetrate to the forest floor. This is why many of the deer and elk like to come in the yard so they can eat grass and clover. Rabbits, quail, and ruffed grouse, as well as the turkeys, love to come in the yard to eat.

To keep from getting cabin fever, Rob and Janet often walk the trails on their property. Rob also must sweep the snow from the solar panels each time they are covered. Maybe the batteries will never run down as does the other things, but he does not want to take the chance. Besides, it gives him something to do.

He and Jan also photograph the many birds and animals. No one will ever see the photos, but they enjoy looking at them on the computer.

Winter seems to drag on, but finally spring is getting close. It is their favorite time of the year and they are looking forward to seeing things grow again.

Chapter 25

The First Year

The weeks have turned into months and the first anniversary finally comes around. The first year has been a year that Rob and Janet will never forget. They have been safe and secure in their tiny island of safety. The outside world, however, is crumbling and disintegrating into ruin and despair. Hundreds of millions have died in wars. Hunger now stalks the entire earth. Many have died from starvation and disease. The very old and feeble were the first to go. Then the sick that could not afford their medication died next. Some parents actually began killing their children if they needed a lot medicine or if they were not very healthy. Nearly every prison had their cell doors opened and tens of thousands of prisoners were released. The reason being, the government could not afford to feed or house the prisoners. If the inmates chose to receive the international number, they were set free. If not, they were quickly put to death or left to die of starvation on the streets.

It was the survival of the fittest. If someone saw a very sick or feeble man, woman or child they were told it was their duty to kill them. This, they said, would leave more food for the rest of the people that needed it. It was dog eat dog world. In fact, people could not afford to feed dogs. Dog food was needed to feed hungry people. Then the dogs became food, as did cats, horses or any animal that moved. Even mice, rats, snakes and lizards were not turned down and were eaten. There were even rumors of cannibalism.

People wondered how it could go on much longer. Yet there were many months left and no one knew how bad it was to get. Even though as bad as it was, people's hearts hardened even more towards God. They blamed him for the evil they had brought on themselves and the evil they were committing.

One night, a few months later, Rob and Janet were watching the local news and they were talking about the drought that had struck the Midwest. The meager crops that had been planted that spring were drying up and dying. Insect pests and diseases had also consumed what the drought hadn't destroyed.

At their home, however, the drought, insects or diseases has not affected them. They are in a different dimension and they soon learn what has happened.

Early one morning, as they are studying the Bible, they go back to the scripture they had read long ago.

Rob is sitting on the front porch swing, reading, as Janet is sitting beside him watching the birds at the feeder and having a cup of coffee.

"Here it is," Rob said. "It's in chapter 12 of Revelation. It says 'The woman fled to the wilderness that God has prepared and there she is nourished for a time, times and dividing of a time.' We are in this *place in the wilderness*—and we have been nourished. Only God could have put us in a different dimension. It says too, that the earth helped the woman. I'm not sure what that means. Whatever it means, it is certain that evil people will not be able to reach those that he is protecting."

Janet looks over at him, "What was that other scripture about ten thousand falling at your side but it will not come near you?"

"I have it written down here on a piece of paper." He then begins flipping through the pages of the Bible trying to find it. "Here it is," he said, as he takes it out and unfolds the sheet of paper. "It's in Psalm 91, 'A thousand shall fall at your side, and ten thousand at your right hand; but it shall not come near you. Only with your eyes, will you look and see the reward of the wicked. Because you have made the Lord, which is my refuge, even the Most High, your habitation. There shall **no evil befall you, neither shall any plague come near your house**. For God shall give his angels charge over you, to keep you in all your ways."

"My Lord, Rob that is what has happened to us. The plagues have not come here because we are protected. Yet we can see the outside world and we know all the terrible things that are happening to those that do not care about God. We also have angels nearby to watch over us."

"There's more, honey," Rob said, as he continues. "It says here, *'He that dwells in the secret place of the Most High shall abide under the shadow of the Almighty. I will say of the Lord, He is my refuge and my fortress: my God; in him will I trust.*

'Surely, he shall deliver you from the snare of the fowler, and from the noisome pestilence. He will cover you with his feathers, and under his wings shall you trust; his truth shall be your shield and buckler. You will not be afraid for the terror by night; or for the arrow that flies by day; nor for the pestilence that walks in darkness; nor for the destruction that waste at noonday.'"

Janet looks up from her cup of coffee, "He is protecting us just like that scripture said."

"Yep, it says, *'He that dwells in the secret place of God will be under his wing.'* We are in *his secret place* and we are under his wing, just like a mother hen protects her young."

"That's what the Lord said about Jerusalem just before he died, remember?"

"Yeah, I remember reading that. He was looking down on Jerusalem and was crying over it because he knew what was going to happen after he was gone. I'll see if I can find it. I think it's in the Gospel of Matthew or maybe Luke."

110

After searching for a few minutes, he finds it. "Here it is. It's in Matthew 23:37, *'How often would I have gathered your children together even as a hen gathers her chickens under her wings, but you would not!'*"

Chapter 26

The Second Year

By the second year, nothing has changed at Rob and Jan's place. The visitors had come for Thanksgiving dinner as they did the first year. They were a welcome sight and it was good to talk to someone. That was the only time they paid them a visit since the last Thanksgiving.

Winter had recently ended and spring is bursting forth. The grass is tall and green once again. The trees are beginning to bud. Soon they will put forth their leaves.

The passenger pigeons came north a couple weeks earlier. An enormous flock had roosted all around their property. They began arriving about an hour before sunset. The sky became black as if by an eclipse of the sun. Rob and Jan sat on the front porch and watched them landing in the forest all around them. They could not hear one another speak because of the deafening roar of the millions of wings. It seemed like a living storm as the pigeon's wings created a strong wind.

As they landed in the nearby forest, they could hear some of the huge limbs breaking from the giant oaks even over the sound of the millions of birds still pouring in. So many pigeons would be landing in the trees that the branches could not hold their enormous weight. Then the limb, along with thousands of birds, would come crashing down, which killed many.

The next day, after they left, it looked as if a hurricane had swept through the woods. Tree branches were all over the ground, along with hundreds of dead birds. The ground was also covered with feathers and was white because of the inch or more of pigeon dung.

The yard was spared most of the feathers, but there were many pigeon droppings because of the birds passing overhead. Rob said it would be good for the grass. It did indeed make the lawn dark green and lush as soon as it rained and soaked the new fertilizer into the roots.

The fruit trees were already blooming and had doubled in size in only one year. Some of the fruit from last year was still stored in the house. Rob and Jan had kept it stored in a box in their utility room, and just like the other food, it never ran out or spoiled.

The past winter was not very cold, but they did have snow quite often. Both of them enjoyed sitting at the kitchen table watching the many kinds of birds that would come to the feeders. They even had some pileated woodpeckers come to the suet feeder and the pair of ivorybills came occasionally. It was amazing to be so close to one of God's spectacular creations. Rob told Jan that when the bird was first discovered it was often called "the Lord God bird". This was because it was so beautiful that when people saw it they would exclaim, "Lord God!" Now there was an evil man calling himself that and trying to rule the world. This one man and his so-called "prophet," were causing all the trouble and heartache that was taking place on the entire earth.

In July of that year, Ron and Janet were walking one of their trails and had stopped to rest. They were sitting on one of the benches Rob had placed beside the path enjoying the peace and quiet of the forest. While sitting there, something out of the corner of their eye gets their attention. Looking up, they the two mysterious men that they now know are angels, coming down the trail towards them. They are wearing their usual attire of buckskin clothes. As they come near, both have smiles. "Hello," Rob said, as he stands and shakes their hands.

"We are sure happy to see you again," Janet said.

"Why is that?" the silver haired man asked.

"We never have company you know."

"Yes, I'm sure it gets a little boring for you with no one else to talk to."

"We have some more questions, if that's alright?" Rob said.

"Yes, what is your question?" asked the silver haired man.

"If we are here in a different dimension, is our house gone back in the dimension we came from?"

"No. It is there. Only you and Janet are gone. The house is there, the land and all that you had is the same as in this place."

"That's strange," Rob said. "What did people think when they saw that we were gone?"

"They just assumed you left and went somewhere else. Later, when it was evident that you weren't returning, many came and took your earthly possessions."

"Well, I suppose I won't ever need them anyway. I have a duplicate copy of everything here," Rob said, with slight laugh.

"That's right," said the dark-haired angel. "You won't ever need them again. And soon you won't need this place."

This concerned Janet somewhat and she asked, "When will that be?"

"No man knows the day or hour, not even the angels in heaven," the dark-haired angel said, with a grin. "You know nearly as much as we do when it comes to that. But you will know when it is getting close, even at the doors."

"You do know that when your clocks stopped, there was a war in heaven?" asked the silver haired man.

"A war in heaven," Janet said, with surprise.

"Yes, didn't you read about it in the book of Revelation? We were there. Lucifer and his angels fought against us and the Most High. That old serpent was thrown out of heaven and down here to earth. That's why all this trouble has come upon humanity. He knows he only has a short time. He and his angels are doing everything in their power to stop God's plan."

"His plan?" Rob said.

"Yes, that God's will be done on earth as it is in heaven. Christ prayed that prayer when his followers asked him how to pray. God's kingdom is coming to earth and Christ will rule with a rod of iron for one thousand years. That is when there will finally be peace on earth and good will towards man."

"I remember reading that now. I believe it is at the end of Revelation."

"It was also said by the angels when Christ was born."

"Yeah," the silver haired angel said, "that was a night I will never forget."

"You were there?" Rob said, with shock.

The dark-haired angel then spoke up. "Yeah, he likes to brag sometimes. He was the one that said it to the shepherds."

"Well, I was told to say it," he said back to the other angel.

"I know," he said, with a grin. "Some get the really good assignments."

Rob and Janet are in awe. They are getting a glimpse into the lives of angels. They never even thought about all the things the messengers of God must do.

"We need to be going now," said the dark-haired angel. "We will be back once more to prepare you for the next great event in your lives."

"What's that?" questioned Rob.

"I think you know. If not, just keep reading and studying, and it will come to you." And with that, they turn and begin walking down the trail towards the forest from where they came. "We'll see you later," the silver haired one said as they both look back and wave. A second later, they fade from view.

Chapter 27

The Final Year

The third year has just passed and it is well into summer. Rob and Jan know things cannot go on much longer. China has been at war and an estimated two billion people have died because of it. They have expanded their country by taking in all the countries around them: Japan, North and South Korea, Vietnam, Cambodia, Thailand, and some of the islands in the Pacific are now part of the Chinese Empire. It seems that they want to take over the world. They boast of having a two-hundred million-man army.

The New Roman Empire has also just about conquered the rest of the world. Only three super-powers remain. Russia is the third. The United States has been attacked from all sides, as was Great Britain. The great cities of New York, Chicago, Los Angeles, Miami, and London, England, now lay in ruins and are all but empty. The streets are impassible because of the skyscrapers and other buildings that have tumbled to earth. The largest cities had nuclear weapons destroy them. Smaller cities and towns were bombed by conventional weapons until they were laid waste.

One third of the people have been killed by the relentless bombings in both countries. One third has died from disease and starvation. The final third has been taken as slaves.

Tiny Israel stands alone as the only place that has so far been spared. The main reason is because the New Temple is there and it is not to be harmed. "Rex Maximus," as he called himself, has plans for Jerusalem. This ancient city is to be his worldwide headquarters where he will someday rule the entire earth.

Unknown to Rob and Jan, this self-proclaimed "god" has plans to attack the other two super-powers. He has heard rumors that China and Russia are going to come to the Middle East and stake their claim to it for the rich oil reserves that are there. He knows whoever owns the oil will control the economy of the world.

Needless to say, there are no more television broadcasts in what was once the United States. All the stations have been destroyed or shut down. They have no way of knowing what is happening in the outside world except for reading the Bible. Those on the outside, however, know what is happening and will see everything unfold as it is written. The two witnesses are soon to meet in Jerusalem. Once there, they will also meet their death. The world will see their bodies lying in the street and will not bury them. A worldwide holiday will be declared and people will be giving gifts to one another. They will be dancing in the streets and having parties because these men tormented them with their preaching and by the many plagues. Yes, people from all over the world will rejoice and think their troubles are over for three and a half days. Then these two witnesses of God will stand to their feet and be caught up into the sky. Great fear will sweep over the earth because of what is coming next. These men warned the world but they did not listen. Now what they said is about to happen, for this will be just before everything ends at Armageddon!

Just as the scriptures in Matthew 24, Mark 13 and Luke 21 had predicted, it is the worst trouble the world has ever seen. It will have to end soon because it won't be long before the three super-powers will annihilate one another and everyone else with them. The human race is near a crossroads. It seems that the leaders are determined to rush headlong into a global war. It will be a war, however, that no one can win. Because of this they will, with their own hand, soon cause the extinction of humanity.

Rob and Jan had stopped watching television a few weeks before the stations were destroyed or shut down. It so depressed them that they could not sleep. They knew they could not stop what was happening and they knew it had to come to pass. They have read and now understand that God is allowing people to reap what they have sown. He has given them free will and the attitude of the majority is that they do not want God in their lives. They think they know more than God does and they are hell bent on destroying the earth and all life from it, just to prove they are right.

Chapter 28

Time is Running Out!

It has now been nearly forty months since Rob and Jan awakened to the day that time stood still. The only way they know what day it is, is by keeping track by updating the calendar they had three years earlier. As said, they stopped watching the news long ago because it was too depressing. They cannot now watch it because there are no more broadcast and haven't been for months.

There is death and destruction all over the world. Wars have killed over half the people on earth and still the wars go on. Hundreds of millions have died by disease and starvation. Many have also been put to death because of their religious beliefs. No one knows what is next, but they know it will not last much longer.

Rob and Janet are sitting on the front porch swing having a cup of coffee after breakfast and just enjoying the mid-summer day.

"It's a beautiful day," Janet said.

"It is," Rob agreed. "It's cool for July."

As they were discussing the weather, they both look up and see the two visitors coming towards them. They haven't seen them for many months.

"Good morning," Rob said, as they neared.

"Good morning," said the silver haired man.

"We haven't seen you for a good while," Rob said. "We thought perhaps you had forgotten about us."

The men smiled. "No, that is not the case. We have come to tell you something important. It will be our last visit."

"Your last visit?" questioned Janet.

"Yes, we will not be needed much longer."

"Why is that?" Rob asked.

"Because you two will not be here much longer."

"Where are we going?" Janet asked, with concern.

"Don't you know?" said the dark-haired man.

"No, not for sure," Rob replied. "I suppose God will take us somewhere else, but we're not sure where."

"You have part of it right," he said. "At this moment, God is pouring out his anger on an evil world. He is doing it to punish the wicked and to try to turn some of the people from their wicked ways to him. It will soon be over."

The other angel then said, "We do not know the day or the hour that God will send for you, but we know it must be within a few weeks—maybe in a few days."

"Days?" Janet said.

"It very well could be," said the dark-haired angel.

"You said God will send for us. How will he do that?" Rob asked.

"When he is ready, he will come to earth and send out his angels to gather all of his people to him. We will not be among the angels that have that responsibility. Each of you will have two angels that are assigned just to you. They will appear and take you to meet Christ."

"Are you talking about the rapture?" Janet asked.

"Many call it that. It is the resurrection of those that have made it into God's kingdom; it is called the first resurrection. Those that are alive and worthy to go with the ones resurrected will also be taken to meet Christ."

"Where will Christ be?" Janet asked.

"Haven't you read that he will be in the air?"

"I've read that," Rob said. "But what happens then?"

"Read Psalm 68:17 and you will know."

The angel then looks at both of them. "I want to make it clear to you that when your change comes it will be as a flash of light. You will be here as mortal beings and in less than a second you will be immortal."

"Immortal?" Janet said.

"Yes, for flesh and blood cannot inherit God's kingdom. As Apostil Paul once said, 'As we have borne the image of the earthly, we shall also bear the image of the heavenly. Flesh and blood cannot inherit the kingdom of God; neither does corruption inherit incorruption. Behold, I will show you a mystery. We shall not all die, but we shall all be changed. In a moment, in the twinkling of an eye, at the last trump: for the trumpet shall sound and the dead shall be raised incorruptible, and we shall be changed. For this corruptible must put on incorruption, and this mortal must put on immortality.'"

Rob and Janet just stand and look at these two beings that speak as if they had heard the words spoken by Paul himself. Then they realize they probably have.

"There is one other thing you two should know," said the silver haired angel. "When you are changed into immortal beings, you will be neither male nor female. You will no longer be married."

"Not be married," Janet said and Rob can hear the disappointment in her voice.

"No, you will be as we are. You will be as the angels in heaven. You will still love one another and know one another, but it will be a different kind of love. You will have spiritual bodies so you will no longer be able to be one together in a physical way."

"You will not miss it," the dark-haired angel said. "You will have no desire and your joy will be so great that sexual intimacy will be the last thing on your mind. We did want to tell you this, however, so you can enjoy the next days or weeks as husband and wife."

"Yes, you have much to look forward to. So, lift up your heads and rejoice because your redemption is drawing near," the silver haired angel said.

Rob and Janet are somewhat stunned. They hardly know what to say. They are both happy and sad at the same time. Happy that it will soon be over, but sad because they will no longer have a close physical relationship they have enjoyed.

"Everything will be fine," the silver haired angel said. "Just take care because you will not know what hour Christ will come, but it will be soon."

Rob was going to ask another question but as he started to speak, the angels looked at them, smiled and began fading before their eyes.

Rob and Janet just sit there staring at the porch where the two visitors once stood. Finally, after several long seconds, Rob turns to Janet. "Well, we know some of what to expect. I suppose we need to get ready for what's coming."

Janet has tears in her eyes. "I can't help but feel sad that we will not be together soon. I love when you hold me and make love to me."

"I love it, too, sweetheart. I guess we will have to take each day as if it will be our last and enjoy one another. That's what we should do every day anyway."

"I know," Janet said. "I will love you with all my heart until the moment the angels come for us."

Rob then remembers what the angel said about Psalm 68. "I'm going in the house and look up that scripture."

"You mean the one the angel said was about where we will be taken?"

"Yes," he said, as he gets up and goes in the house. "I'll be right back." A minute later, he comes back onto the porch and has the Bible opened to Psalms. "What was that, Psalms 68, what?"

"I believe he said 68:17," Janet replied.

"I found it," Rob said and he begins reading aloud, "The chariots of God are twenty thousand, even thousands upon thousands and the Lord is among them."

"What does that mean, Rob?"

"It means that Christ is coming to earth from heaven in what the Bible calls chariots. It is what we today would call spaceships, millions of them!"

Epilogue

When I began this book, I had no idea how it would come together. The more I wrote, the clearer things became. Right after I began the story, I remembered a line from a scripture and looked it up. To my amazement, it was in Psalm 91. When Satan was trying to tempt Christ, he quoted from this same Psalm. It was when Satan took him up to a high place at the temple and told him to jump. Satan knew the scripture said that Christ would be protected from harm. If he jumped with people around and did not fall to his death, but was caught by angels, people would know he was one of God's prophets. Christ told Satan, however, he would not temp God by doing such a thing.

When I began reading Psalm 91, I also saw several parallels to what is said in Revelation 12:14 about the "woman" being given two wings of an eagle where she flies into the wilderness and is protected and nourished for a "time, times and dividing of a time." God said in Psalm 91, "He that dwells in *the secret place* of the Most High shall abide under the shadow of the Almighty." He also said, "A thousand shall fall at your side, and ten thousand at your right hand; but it shall not come near you. Only with your eyes, will you look and see the reward of the wicked. Because you have made the Lord, which is my refuge, even the most High, your habitation. There shall no evil befall you, **neither shall any plague come near your house**. For God shall give his angels charge over you, to keep you in all your ways."

I have never heard anyone even try to explain where or what the meaning of this "place in the wilderness" is in Revelation 12:6 and 12:14. The Bible said that God prepares this "place" and the woman, which is a symbol of God's church, is there for three and a half years. No one knows if this "place" is a literal place on earth of if it is speaking figuratively of God just protecting those he deems worthy. There are only two other scriptures that mention this protection. The first is in Luke 21:35 when Christ said, "Pray that your will be *worthy to escape these things* (the Great Tribulation). The Second scripture is in Revelation 3:10 where it says, "Since you have kept my command to endure patiently, *I will also keep you from the hour of trial* that is going to come upon the whole world to test those who live on the earth."

Many today believe that God will "rapture" his church from the earth before the Tribulation and take them to heaven. This is written nowhere in the Bible. On the contrary, it says the very opposite! I have written several books about the coming of the Lord and the resurrection or as most know it, the "rapture". One is titled, "A Rude Awaking". I have studied End Time prophecies for over fifty years. It would take much too long to give all the scriptures to explain it, but this is exactly why most will not be worthy to escape. They have been deceived into a false sense of security. Those that do not teach the truth will be the leading cause of why "As a snare it shall come upon the whole world to test everyone living," Luke 21:35 and Revelation 3:10.

No one knows where this "secret place" is that God has prepared but I myself believe it is an actual place. I also believe that it will be much like what I have described in this fictional book. I believe this because of what God did in the past to protect and supply the needs of his people. I used what happened to the children of Israel while they were in the wilderness for forty years. Deuteronomy 29:5, "During the forty years that I led you through the desert, your clothes did not wear out, nor did the sandals on your feet."

The gasoline never running out, as well as all their food, was because of what happened to the prophet Elijah during the three and a half years that he was used of God. He stayed with a widow woman and her son and God kept them from starving. 1 Kings 17:14-16, "For thus says the Lord God of Israel, 'The barrel of meal shall not waste, neither shall the cruse of oil fail, until the day that the Lord sends rain upon the earth.'

"And she went and did according to the saying of Elijah: and she, and he, and her house, did eat many days. And the barrel of meal wasted not, neither did the cruse of oil fail, according to the word of the Lord, which he spoke by Elijah."

The trees that bear fruit on trees that are too young, came from what happened to Aaron's staff. Numbers 17:8, "And it came to pass, that on the morrow Moses went into the tabernacle of witness; and, behold, the rod of Aaron for the house of Levi was budded, and brought forth buds, and bloomed blossoms, and yielded almonds."

Rob and Jan were healed from all diseases because of what happened to the Israelites when they came out of Egypt. "There was not one feeble person among them," Psalm 105:37.

The event I described of the Mercy Seat, having the blood of Christ on it, is based on what Ron Wyatt has testified to. Ron Wyatt was a famous archeologist and one with much Christian faith. He has since died, but when alive, he claimed that he found the Ark under where Christ was crucified.

Above the hidden cave where the Arks rest, is a place several feet wide and several feet high that is set back into a rock wall a few feet. Here there are four, four-inch square holes that have been carved into the bottom rock where beams were placed for the crucifixion of criminals during the time of The Roman Empire in the first century. In front of one the holes, is a large crack where the blood and water that gushed forth from Christ's side ran down and dripped onto the Mercy Seat when He died and there was an earthquake, Matthew 27:50-51: "Jesus, when he had cried again with a loud voice, yielded up the ghost. And, behold, the veil of the temple was rent (or torn) in two from the top to the bottom; and the earth did quake, and **the rocks** *were* **rent**."

There are several videos of Ron Wyatt online that he and others have made. I believe this to be true, because only God could have had the Ark placed below where Christ was to die hundreds of years in advance. Christ became our High Priest and he would have likely put his blood on the Mercy Seat to atone for the sins of the world. Why else would God have had a temple made in the first place to house the Ark if it was not of the utmost importance? Inside the Ark are the "Ten Commandments" or God's words. Christ is the "Word of God." John 1:1 &14, "In the beginning was the Word, and the Word was with God, and the Word was God. And the Word was made flesh and dwelt among us."

When you write a book and create characters, you become attached to them. You give them a personality, problems to overcome and you actually begin to care about a fictional person that does not truly exist. I can only imagine how we must be to God. We are not just fictional charters He created for a story, but we are His creations and He cares about our every need. I hope you enjoyed my story about the day that time stood still. Thank you.

Why the Book was Written

I have had the idea for this book for many years. At first, I only had the part of the house being inside a bubble of a different time. I thought it would be a good story if all around the couple there would be birds and animals of long ago. I even thought about going back further so there would be mammoths or even dinosaurs.

Here is an insight of another reason I wrote this book. Some of the story is actually true about the animals coming to Rob and Janet's cabin. There is an old box turtle as I described. She comes several times each summer and will eat from our hand. She is so old that her markings are nearly gone. A photo of her is at the end of this book.

I have also reached down and touched young fence lizards as they lay resting and they did not move. Once, when I was digging in my garden, I dug up some fence lizard eggs. Placing them in a container of dirt, I hatched them. They were very tame even after I turned them loose on a nearby rock pile. I would often go out and watch them from just a couple of feet away. Even today, my wife, Lilly and I can sit on the front porch and fence lizards will be just a few feet away. They pay little attention to us. Even the five-lined skinks come within a few feet and show little fear.

In the summer of 2016, we had a family of raccoons that was coming to the house looking for something to eat. They were so tame they would take food from our hand. The year before, we had a raccoon we named "Stubby" come and she, too, would take food from our hand. Her photo is also at the end of this book. We called her Stubby because she was missing the end of her tail.

The most amazing thing to happen, however, was what happened with a wild grey fox. Several years ago, we had at least two coming to the house and eating cat food from our front porch. The food was for Buddy and Rambo the two orphaned raccoons we were raising. We saw them often and I wondered what one would do if I caught it. Therefore, after locking the chickens and pigeons in their house, I put a screen door spring on the chicken coop door. Then tying a string to a stick, which held the door open, I ran it to a window in the house. I then put some scraps of meat on the ground leading to inside the pen. Then, just before dark, one of the foxes showed up. After finding the trail of meat, he proceeded to eat as he walked right into the coop. I quickly pulled the string and the door slammed shut behind the unsuspecting fox. Then as expected, the fox ran around the pen crashing into the wire trying to get out.

Rushing outside, I neared the pen expecting the fox to try even harder to get out, but to my surprise, he ran towards me, climbed the wire and sat on a limb I had put in the corner of the coop so my pigeons could perch on it. I had heard of Gray Foxes climbing trees, but had never seen it myself. That was not the most surprising thing it did, however. Expecting the fox to go wild with fear as I approached, it instead sat there looking at me. "This is incredible," I thought. "Why doesn't it act afraid?" Then to my utter amazement, I took a piece of meat it had missed and putting it to the wire the fox took it from my hand! I saw what was happening, but I still could not believe it. Calling my wife outside so she could be witness to this extraordinary event, she too fed the wild fox from her hand. If someone would have told me of this I would not have believed it. It happened, I saw it and I still have a hard time believing it.

The Beasts of the Wild

Below are some of the wild creatures that have come to our cabin. A photo of the cabin is also at the end of this book. I have written another book about my life as a writer and how God's unseen hand guided me in following that dream when it seemed impossible. It is titled, "A Cabin in the Woods".

A baby fence lizard on our front porch. Beside it is the head of a 16-penny nail.

This is the very old female Box Turtle. She has just about lost all her markings on her shell. She has looked this way for at least the last twenty years because that is when I first saw her. I would guess she is around seventy to eighty years old and may be much older. She has been coming to the house each year for watermelon and cantaloupe, which we feed her. Here she is dining on a piece of beef sausage and strawberry tops.

Stubby was a wild raccoon, with a bobbed tail, that came to our front door each night wanting food. She became tame enough to take cookies from our hand. Here she is eating cat food on the front porch as I stand beside her taking the photo.

Above is a mother raccoon and her young that are coming to the house for something to eat. The young ones would take food from our hand. I do not advise anyone to do this unless you are very familiar with the animals and know that they can become dependent on handouts. We only did this a few times and stopped.

"You will have a covenant with the stones of the field and the wild animals will be at peace with you," Job 5:23.

About the Author

Kenneth Edward Barnes has been called, *"A modern day Mark Twain"* by a local newspaper reporter. *"He shows a Twain sense of humor in conversation and in his writing. He writes in the 'down to earth' style that Twain used to capture the heart of America."*

He was born on April 4, 1951, along the banks of Little Pigeon Creek in the southern tip of Indiana, downstream from where Abraham Lincoln grew up. As a child, he loved fishing from the muddy banks of the creek and roaming in the nearby woods. He never missed an opportunity to be in the outdoors where he could see all of God's creation.

Ken is a nationally published writer, poet and the author of over one hundred books. Some of his most popular ones are: *The Mammoth Slayers; A Cabin in the Woods;*

Mysteries of the Bible; Madam President; Life Along Little Pigeon Creek; A Children's Story Collection; The Golden Sparrow; Buddy and Rambo: The Orphaned Raccoons; Outdoor Adventures; The Arkansas River Monster collection, and *Do Pets go to Heaven?* This could soon change, however, as he has recently written several others.

The author became a member of *Hoosier Outdoor Writers* in 1993, where he has won several awards from them in their annual writing contest. He has also been a guest speaker for the *Boy Scouts, Daughters of the American Revolution, Teachers Reading Counsel, Kiwanis Club*, and at several schools, libraries and churches.

Ken has been an outdoor columnist and contributing editor for several newspapers and magazines: *Ohio Valley Sportsman, Kentucky Woods and Waters, Southern Indiana Outdoors, Fur-Fish-Game, Wild Outdoor World, Mid-West Outdoors,* and a hard cover book titled *From the Field.* He has written for the *Boonville Standard, Perry County News, Newburgh Register and Chandler Post.* He has had poems published locally and nationally. One titled *The Stranger* went to missionaries around the world. The poem, *Princess,* was also published locally and nationally, and won honorable mention in a national contest. His best-loved poem is *Condemned* and has been published by the tens of thousands. Nearly every single poem he has written is in his colored paperback book, *Poems from the Heart* and *My Favorite Poems.*

Ken has worked for an Evansville, Indiana, television station where he had outdoor news segments aired that he wrote, directed and edited. He also had film clips that were aired on the national television shows *Real TV* and *Animal Planet.* At this time, he has several short videos on YouTube and on GodTube.

Studying nature since childhood, he is a self-taught ornithologist and a conservationist. In 2009, he became founder and president of the *Golden Sparrow Nature Society*, the name of which was chosen because of his first published book. Ken loves to share his knowledge and love of nature, and it has been said that he is a walking encyclopedia on birds and animals. Because of this, he recently published an e-book titled *Birds and Animals of Southern Indiana*. It has over 300 photos of birds and animals, most of which he photographed himself. He frequently updates it with new photos.

He has followed his dream of being a writer since 1978 and now lives in a cabin in the woods. Being an individualist, he cleared the land, dug a well by hand and built the house himself, which uses only solar electric. He even wrote a book titled *Solar Electric: How does that work?*

Comments on the author's work can be left on his Facebook page at: **Kenneth Edward Barnes**, or on **Twitter** at **Kenneth Edward Barne @BarneKenneth.** All of Ken's books can be seen on his **Author Page** at Amazon.

Books by Kenneth Edward Barnes in:
Paperback, Hardcover and E-book

1. In Search of a Golden Sparrow
2. Life on Pigeon Creek
3. Barnestorming the Outdoors
4. Invasion of the Dregs
5. A Children's Story Collection
6. Poems from the Heart
7. The B.O.O.K. (Bible Of Observational Knowledge)
Under the pen name of ZTW

Books available as E-books only:

1. Is There a Devil? Is Satan Real?
2. The Thirteenth Disciple
3. The Two Witnesses
4. The Mammoth Slayers: Why the series was written
5. Birds and Animals of Southern Indiana
6. The Ancient Art of Falconry
7. Solar Electric: How does that work?
8. Instruction Manual for the WIFE (Wonderful Idea From Eden)

9. How to Care for your MAN (Mate's Animalistic Needs)
10. How to Raise your CHILD (Cute Huggable Innocent Little Darling)
11. INSTINCTS (Interesting Nature Secret Tendencies If Nature Could Teach Secrets)
12. The Adventures of Ralph and Fred
13. Twelve Tantalizing Tongue Twisting Tales
14. The Last Mammoth
15. A Squirrel Named Rufus
16. Pete: The Poor Pig
17. The Bike Ride
18. The Great Yankeetown Easter Egg Hunt
19. King and Tippy: Two Special Puppies
20. The Wanderer of Little Pigeon Creek
21. The Panther
22. A Legend Comes Alive
23. The Eagle and the Hummingbird
24. The Grumbling Grasshopper
25. Buzz: The Cowfly
26. The Watermelon Turtle
27. I Don't want to be a Pig!
28. Who? What? When? Where? Why?
29. Buggies: (Also, includes: Animal Cracks and other jokes and riddles)

Available as Paperback and E-books:

1. A Biblical Mystery: Christians need to become a Jew: What does this mean?
2. A Cabin in the Woods
3. A Day Appointed
4. A House Divided: This is why Donald Trump won the election
5. A Rude Awakening
6. Abortion: Why all the controversy?
7. Betrayed
8. Beyond the Grave: Is there life after death?

45. The Arkansas River Monster
46. The Arkansas River Monster: The complete series
47. The Black Widow
48. The Book of HUMOR
49. The Book of WISDOM (Words Instructing Spiritual Direction Of Man)
50. The Capture of the Arkansas River Monster
51. The Coming Invasion
52. The Creature of O'Minee
53. The Day that Time Stood Still
54. The Five Dimensions of Sex
55. The Golden Sparrow
56. The Last Arkansas River Monster
57. The Long Pond Road
58. The Invasion of the Dregs
59. The Mammoth Slayers
60. The Mammoth Slayers: Last Clan of Neanderthals
61. The Mammoth Slayers: The Last Neanderthal
62. The Mammoth Slayers: The Prequel
63. The Mammoth Slayers: The Trilogy
64. The Ruby Ring and the Impossible Dream
65. The Unexplained
66. The War on Christians
67. The Words and Life of Jesus
68. Thou Shall Not Kill: What does God think about the killing of animals?
69. To Keep a Secret
70. What in the World is Wrong?
71. Why Does God Let Bad Things Happen?
72. Words to Live By

Made in the USA
Las Vegas, NV
16 September 2021

30411483R00079